Praise for *Power Forward,*
On Point, and *Bounce Back*

"Zayd is a sympathetic protagonist, and his story is told with humor and artfully filled with interesting cultural matter . . . . Readers will cheer for Zayd."
—*Kirkus Reviews* on *Power Forward*

"A great pick for elementary-age readers . . . .
A delightful follow-up from a writer who understands children, family, and culture."
—*Kirkus Reviews* on *On Point*

"A great balance between sports action and realistic fiction . . . . Readers will look forward to further adventures featuring Zayd."
—*Booklist* on *On Point*

"Fast-paced but never rushed, Khan deftly ties together larger themes of teamwork, friendship, and standing up for oneself . . . . An excellent sports series."
—*School Library Journal* on *On Point*

"A solid read about being your best self on and off the court."
—*Kirkus Reviews* on *Bounce Back*

Praise for Hena Khan

★ "Amina's middle school woes and the universal themes running through the book transcend culture, race, and religion."
—*Kirkus Reviews* on *Amina's Voice*, starred review

★ "A universal story of self-acceptance and the acceptance of others. A welcome addition to any middle grade collection."
—*School Library Journal* on *Amina's Voice*, starred review

★ "Written as beautifully as Amina's voice surely is, this compassionate, timely novel is highly recommended for all libraries."
—*Booklist* on *Amina's Voice*, starred review

★ "Khan nimbly incorporates details of modern life and allusions to Alcott's classic."
—*Publishers Weekly* on *More to the Story*, starred review

"Comfortingly familiar yet also entirely new, like an old friend given a makeover . . . . A delightful concept well executed, this volume is sure to find many fans."
—*Kirkus Reviews* on *More to the Story*

ALSO BY HENA KHAN

Amina's Voice

It's Ramadan, Curious George

Golden Domes and Silver Lanterns:
A Muslim Book of Colors

Night of the Moon: A Muslim Holiday Story

Under My Hijab

More to the Story

ZAYD SALEEM, CHASING THE DREAM

HENA KHAN

ILLUSTRATED BY
SALLY WERN COMPORT

SALAAM
R E A D S
NEW YORK | LONDON | TORONTO
SYDNEY | NEW DELHI

⬡ SALAAM
   READS

An imprint of Simon & Schuster Children's Publishing Division
1230 Avenue of the Americas, New York, New York 10020
This book is a work of fiction. Any references to historical events, real people, or real places are used fictitiously. Other names, characters, places, and events are products of the author's imagination, and any resemblance to actual events or places or persons, living or dead, is entirely coincidental.
Power Forward, *On Point*, and *Bounce Back* text © 2018 by Hena Khan
Cover illustrations copyright © 2020 by Alessia Trunfio
Interior illustrations copyright © 2018 by Sally Wern Comport
All rights reserved, including the right of reproduction in whole or in part in any form.
SALAAM READS and its logo are trademarks of Simon & Schuster, Inc.
For information about special discounts for bulk purchases, please contact Simon & Schuster Special Sales at 1-866-506-1949 or business@simonandschuster.com.
The Simon & Schuster Speakers Bureau can bring authors to your live event. For more information or to book an event, contact the Simon & Schuster Speakers Bureau at 1-866-248-3049 or visit our website at www.simonspeakers.com.
Also available in a Salaam Reads hardcover edition
Interior design by Dan Potash
Cover design by Krista Vossen
The text for this book was set in Iowan Old Style.
The illustrations for this book were rendered in Prismacolor pencil on Denril and digital.
Manufactured in the United States of America
First Simon & Schuster Books for Young Readers paperback edition August 2020
0720 OFF
10 9 8 7 6 5 4 3 2 1
Library of Congress Cataloging-in-Publication Data
Names: Khan, Hena, author. | Comport, Sally Wern, illustrator. | Khan, Hena. Power forward. | Khan, Hena. On point. | Khan, Hena. Bounce back.
Title: Zayd Saleem, chasing the dream / Hena Khan ; illustrated by Sally Wern Comport.
Description: New York : Simon & Schuster, [2020] | Audience: Ages 7 to 12. | Audience: Grades 2–3. | Summary: Collects three stories, previously published separately, about Zayd, who gains the support of his family and friends to pursue his dream of becoming a star player on his middle school basketball team.
Identifiers: LCCN 2020011290 | ISBN 9781534469471 (hardcover) | ISBN 9781534469464 (paperback)
Subjects: CYAC: Basketball—Fiction. | Pakistani American—Fiction. | Family life—Fiction. | Middle schools—Fiction. | Schools—Fiction.
Classification: LCC PZ7.K52652 Zay 2020 | DDC [Fic]—dc23
LC record available at https://lccn.loc.gov/2020011290

POWER FORWARD

For Farrukh

ACKNOWLEDGMENTS

Writing this series, which was like winning a championship game to me, was only possible because of the wonderful team that helped it come to life. My super-smart and insightful agent, Matthew Elblonk, signed me with the awesome Salaam Reads team. Coach Zareen Jaffery shared my passion for the series and used her expert editing skills to bring out the best in these books, along with the vision of Dan Potash and the design group at Simon & Schuster. I'm lucky to work out with talented trainers, including Ann McCallum, Joan Waites, Laura Gehl, Afgen Sheikh, and Andrea Menotti, who pushed me to exercise my writing muscles and offered invaluable advice. I also have the best fans in the world: my beloved parents, siblings, and friends. Thank you for cheering me on throughout life, and for inspiring characters that might resemble you at times. And finally, my incredible teammates: my husband, Farrukh, and sons, Bilal and Humza, not only lived many of the experiences in this series but also helped me to weave them into a story with humor and heart—and the right basketball terminology.

You will forever be my MVPs.

I've imagined lots of ways to get famous. The best of all would be if I took a game-winning shot in the NBA finals. But I wouldn't mind being a magician who slices people in half on *America's Got Talent*. I'd like to set the Guinness World Record for burping the Chinese alphabet. I've seen lots of YouTube videos. I know what it takes to become famous.

I never, ever, imagined getting famous by playing the violin at the Brisk River Elementary School fall concert.

The concert program booklet calls it a "memorable night of musical escape." The sweaty audience slumped on rows of metal folding chairs looks ready to escape. It feels like three hundred degrees in the school cafeteria. But "memorable"? I'm sure everyone will forget tonight as soon as they rush out the doors to the parking lot.

Ms. Sterling is waving her baton like she's conducting the National Symphony Orchestra, not the fourth-grade orchestra. I'm sitting on the second level of the stage, melting in a white shirt, black pants, and purple clip-on bow tie. It's extra hot because I'm wearing my basketball

training jersey and shorts underneath. I ran over from the gym right after practice. And I couldn't find my dress shoes this morning, so I'm in my sneakers. My basketball and empty water bottle are tucked under my chair.

Our third song goes perfectly. Ms. Sterling raises her hands, soaking in the applause. Next is our finale, "Tribal Lament." It ends with a cool drum solo by Antonio. I raise my violin to my chin. Abigail, who's sitting next to me, starts to whisper.

"Zayd! I need more room." She sticks her bow out so far that it almost touches my face.

"See?" she whines. "Move over!"

I scoot my chair to the right a few inches and start playing.

"I need more room!" Abigail hisses.

It looks like Abigail has plenty of room, but she's glaring at me. So I scoot over again, way over to the edge of the riser. I shift in my seat, still playing, and then—oh no! My chair tips over and I'm falling. AHHHHH!

I see my life flashing before my eyes. Wait, no. Phew. It's the flashes of everyone's cameras. And then, CRASH! I land smack in the middle of the drums, barely missing Antonio. My chair clangs to the floor somewhere behind me. WHACK! My basketball smacks me on the head before bouncing into the audience.

All the music stops. I hear gasps from the crowd. Then there's nothing but silence. Ms. Sterling rushes over to me, her face pale.

"Zayd! Are you okay? Can you move?" she shrieks.

I nod, take her hand, and slowly stand up. My shirt is untucked and a little torn, and my bright red training jersey is peeking through. My bow tie is missing. But nothing seems broken, especially not my playing arms. For playing *basketball*, I mean. I can't afford to be injured. My league has tryouts coming up in just four weeks, and I have to make the gold team.

Ms. Sterling looks like she's about to cry. I can feel everyone's eyes fixed on me. And then, suddenly, I understand what "the show must go on" means.

I face the audience and take an extra-deep bow. Everyone cheers, whistles, and applauds. And then I actually get . . . a STANDING OVATION! I bow again and can't help but laugh with the crowd. I rub my head where the basketball hit me, and someone from the audience throws it back to me.

As I climb back onto the risers, Abigail helps me set up my chair.

"Sorry," she mumbles.

If you had told me I was going to be famous today, I wouldn't have believed it. My older sister Zara posted a video of my fall on YouTube. It's already been viewed forty thousand times. In six hours! I can only imagine how famous I'll be by tomorrow. And in the end, this concert might actually be memorable after all.

2

Today I'm on fire. Not on fire as in "stop, drop, and roll." On fire as in *completely unstoppable* on the basketball court.

It's almost the end of practice, and I've got a steal, six baskets, and four rebounds. All the soreness I felt the day after I fell off the stage is gone. Right now I feel amazing. This is my best scrimmage of the season.

"Stop standing!" Coach shouts. Alex and his headband dribble past four of us to score an easy layup.

I inbound the ball and run down the court. Sweat is dripping onto my face. Alex looks cool in a headband, but Zara says they make me look like a dork. So I wipe the sweat onto my sleeve.

I yank up my shorts as I run. My mom had to sew in a tighter elastic, like with most of my shorts, since the drawstring doesn't pull. I don't understand why they make gym shorts with fake strings that hang there, like lost shoelaces that don't actually *do* anything.

Chris throws me the ball past half-court, and I dribble with my left hand. I cross over to my right to get by a defender. Then I pass it to

Keanu and . . . SWISH! He hits an easy shot from right outside the paint.

Coach is nodding now, and he mutters, "All right, all right." That's like hearing "good job" from someone who actually praises kids. Not Coach. He groans extra loud, clamps his hands over his head, and screams at us from the sideline. Mama says he must sweat out five pounds during our games. But I get it.

Coach Wheeler lives for basketball, like me. Plus, he makes us work hard. In my old league we had a super-nice coach. But all we got was a sportsmanship award after losing every game by twenty points or more. This season I'm playing better. And we've been winning, too.

"Nice pass," Keanu says to me after Coach blows the whistle.

Coach blows the whistle again, and I

inbound the ball. William dribbles down to the three-point line and passes to Chris. I pause, and my brain goes into overdrive. It's like I'm seeing everything in slow motion. I've been hot today. What better way to end the scrimmage, and impress Coach, than by taking a winning shot?

I glance over at Keanu, and then, instead of setting a screen, call for the ball. Chris passes it to me. I'm feeling confident as I dribble, pump fake, and launch a shot that goes straight into the hoop.

SIZZLE.

Did I mention I'm on fire?

Coach kind of half smiles at me when I pass him to grab my water bottle from the bench. My heart beats quicker as I imagine playing this well during tryouts. If I do, I have a real chance at moving up from the D league to the gold team.

My best friend Adam is on the gold team, and it's my dream for the two of us to play together. Plus I hate the way D league sounds. I know the *D* stands for "developmental," but it's always felt like a bad grade or something. I'm ready to go for the gold.

3

My dad says that good things come always in threes. Number 1: I had an awesome practice. Number 2: I spot my grandmother's car with a giant gold-and-green "ALLAH" medallion hanging from the rearview mirror. It pulls up in the pickup lane. I can't wait to see what number three will be.

Naano isn't like grandmothers you see on TV. She doesn't smother me with hugs, bake me cookies, or say things like "bless your heart." She won't let me shake her hand until I wash mine first. The only cookies in her house come in crinkly packages. And her favorite sayings are curses in Urdu. In other words, she's awesome.

"Mama's still in meeting. You win?" she asks as I crawl into the back seat. The car smells like cardamom and muscle rub.

"Yeah, but it was just practice," I say. "Not a real game."

"Humph. Win next game. You will."

It's a statement. Like she knows the future. Naano kind of speaks like Yoda.

We get to her house, and my grandfather, Nana Abu, is napping. That means Naano can focus on feeding me. The only thing she's more obsessed with than the perfect cup of chai is how to fatten up "skinny mouse." That's her nickname for me.

"Paratha?" she asks. Before I open my mouth, she uncovers a bowl draped with a towel and pulls off a chunk of dough. Even though she shuffles when she walks, her hands move with lightning speed. I wish I could dribble as fast as she rolls out the dough into a perfect flat circle. She slices butter into it, folds it up, rolls it out again, and puts it on a pan. I watch it sizzle and bubble up, and realize I'm starving.

"Sugar?" Naano doesn't wait for an answer again. The paratha is resting on a plate. She smears more butter on top, sprinkles it with sugar, and hands it to me.

I devour it while Naano watches me with

a satisfied smile on her face. This was nothing like the baked veggie chips and healthy granola bars that Mama's been giving me for snacks lately.

"Milk? You need milk," she says. She starts to get up to go to the fridge.

"No thanks, Naano, I don't like milk." As I say the words, Naano slumps back in her chair. It's like I've personally insulted her. But my stomach hurts when I drink milk. Or maybe I just don't like it. I'm not sure.

My mom wants me to keep track of the things I eat and what makes my stomach hurt. She said that way we can figure out if something is wrong with me, like an allergy or something. That's when Zara said, "There's definitely something wrong with you," and I pushed her, and Mama yelled at us both for fighting.

A few days later Mama gave me a notebook called FOOD JOURNAL and wrote on half the pages:

DATE/TIME:

WHAT I ATE:

HOW I FEEL:

I thought she was kidding, but she wasn't. Writing in the journal feels like homework, and I always forget to do it. Plus nobody else I know has to do anything like this.

"Oh, my dramas!" Snack time is over. Naano shuffles to the family room and shakes and mutters at the remote until the TV is on, extra loud.

I used to be able go outside and practice free throws on the old hoop that belonged to my uncle, Jamal Mamoo. But last month my grandfather backed his car into it and it fell over. I pull out a book and pretend to be more interested in it than in Naano's show, *Dil Nahi Chahta*. I watch it every couple of weeks or so when I'm visiting. But the story changes so slowly I can follow along, even though I only speak a few words of Urdu. What I've figured out is:

- ✓ The main character wants to make movies and is always running around with a big camera trying to film people who slam doors in his face.

- ✓ His parents are really mad at him because they want him to be a doctor and marry their best friends' daughter.

- ✓ The camera randomly cuts from one frozen angry face to another around the room while intense music plays.

- ✓ Every three minutes or so there's a commercial break. Most commercials are for cheap flights to India, frozen Indian foods, and some guy named Prem Jyotish who REALLY wants you to call him today.

When I start to laugh because the guy follows an old lady into a fabric store with his camera, and she slams the door in his face, Naano shushes me.

"Where is your mother? Isn't it time for you to go home?" She says it like it could be a joke, but I can't tell for sure.

Naano waits for the next commercial and goes into the kitchen to make chai. And then the doorbell rings.

My mom bursts inside, scanning the room like she's lost something until she sees me. She gives me a tired smile.

"Asalaamualaikum. How was practice, sweetie?" she says. "Sorry. I didn't expect to be so late."

"You want chai? Paratha?" Naano calls out from the kitchen.

"I'm good." Mama turns to Naano. "You

really should watch your diet, Ammi, and stop making parathas. That's a lot of carbs."

"Bakwas," snorts Naano. That's her favorite word. I think it means something like "nonsense," and she says it all the time. "I'll show you carbs."

"Thanks for picking Zayd up." Mama gives Naano a hug. "See you this weekend."

"Next time I make my skinny mouse aloo paratha," Naano says to me with a wink.

Mama shakes her head. Those are parathas stuffed with potatoes. But I can't wait. Good things *do* come in threes, and that paratha was number three.

4

We pull up into the driveway, and who's there, taking free throws? Zara. Ugh. It's not fair. My sister doesn't love basketball like me, but she's amazing at it. She's good at everything she does. And she's done everything, from tae kwon do to gymnastics to basket weaving.

"What's up?" Zara tosses me the ball as I get out of the car. I take a shot, and it hits the rim hard and bounces into the neighbor's yard. In my defense, the rim is a little bent.

"Nothing," I say. I chase after the ball and fling it sideways toward the hoop again. But it smacks the side of the backboard. Then it almost hits me in the face, like a boomerang.

"Nice," Zara says as she grabs and swishes the ball through the net. It's like Zara sucked up all of my good energy from earlier.

"I'm going inside," I say. I grab my stuff from Mama's car and drag it into the house. Maybe Zara isn't trying to show off, but it's still annoying. I know I'm better at basketball than Zara, and better than the D league. I just need to prove it during tryouts.

"Asalaamualaikum, Baba." My father is

back from an overnight trip and is taking off his shoes. He gives me a hug.

"Walaikum asalaam. How was school yesterday?"

"Fine." I can't even remember what happened at school. It feels like ages ago.

"Did you have your math test?"

"Yeah."

Baba keeps looking at me with his eyebrows raised. He wants more detail.

"I did okay, I think. We didn't get it back yet. But, Baba, can we get a new hoop?"

"A what?"

I take a deep breath.

"Our rim's bent, and my shots don't go in. And the height thingy is rusted. Can we get a new basketball hoop? A good one, like Adam's? I need to practice for tryouts."

Baba sighs.

"I just got home. Can we talk about this later?"

"Okay." He didn't say no. I can work with that.

I kick off my shoes and head to my room. There's a framed photo over my bed of John Wall making a behind-the-back pass that Adam got me for my birthday. On my other wall I tacked up a poster of Michael Jordan flying through the air for a slam dunk. Even my comforter that Mama found at a bargain bedding shop has a basketball pattern on it. The threads started coming out after only a few weeks, but I still love it.

If it were up to my mom, my room would look completely different. She suggested a musical theme, with musical-note decals on the walls and violin-decorated bedding.

"How about I make printouts of all your favorite composers?" she said. I'm not even kidding. She thought I'd rather look at a bunch

of old guys in powdered wigs than basketball legends.

"Zayd! Dinner!" Mama calls.

"What's this?" Zara wrinkles her nose as we sit around the table.

"Spinach cakes."

"It's so . . . *green*." Zara pokes her spinach cake with her fork. "Spinach" and "cake" are two words that should never be put together. Like "fart" and "marshmallow." It doesn't sound right.

"Green means filled with vitamins. We need to eat healthier. Try it."

I think about this afternoon's paratha and sigh.

"Zayd, don't forget to practice violin after you shower," Mama says. She scoops salad onto my plate.

"Do we have creamy dressing?" Baba asks. He's also eying his food with suspicion. I imagine the three of us look like a scene from Naano's show, *Dil Nahi Chahta*. The camera would cut to each of our eyes, staring at our plates in fear.

"That's filled with fat and chemicals. Try this olive oil and vinegar," Mama says.

Meals like this are why my grandmother and mother disagree about me. Naano says my mother feeds me "grass," and that's the reason I'm so skinny. She likes to serve me lots of red meat, fried foods, and sugar. When we

go to the grocery store together, Naano even buys me cheddar-jalapeño Cheetos.

Ever since my mom watched some movie about a guy who ate nothing but McDonald's for a month and made himself sick, she decided we all need to eat less junk food. And she acts like Naano is trying to poison me. But if I had to choose which food to be scared of, I'd pick this bright green spinach cake. Cheetos may have seventeen ingredients I can't pronounce. But they look perfect to me. And they taste like spicy little pieces of cheese heaven.

"Why aren't you finishing, Zayd?" Mama frowns.

"My stomach hurts a little." Oops. Now Mama is going to want me to write this down in that food journal. And my stomach doesn't *really* hurt. It just feels a little hungry for something other than spinach cake. Like a new basketball hoop. And making the gold team. And kids putting posters of me up on their walls one day. Some Cheetos wouldn't hurt either.

5

"Bye, Mama!" I jump out of the car and grab my lunch bag and violin. A teacher holds open the door to the school entrance by the gym for me, and I dash inside.

"No running!" he orders. I slow to a run-walk since I'm late for violin practice. The advanced orchestra meets in the mornings before school twice a week. My mom was super excited when Ms. Sterling invited me to join it. She doesn't even complain about having to drive me to school extra early.

As I pass the gym, I hear whistles blowing and peek inside. Adam, Blake, and a couple of other kids from the gold team are there, running up and down the court. I'm so surprised to see them that I stop in my tracks.

"Hey, Zayd!" Adam waves me in.

"What are you doing here?" I ask him. "Don't you guys have practice in the afternoon?"

"Yeah, but we got dropped off early. Mr. Lee says he's in here anyway, so we can use the gym. As long as no one else signs up for it."

"You're so lucky."

"Wanna play?" Adam flicks me the ball, and I grab it. SMACK! My violin case hits the gym floor. I'm glad it's padded inside.

I pause for a moment, holding the ball. What should I do? Play basketball with my friend, or practice scales with Abigail and Ms. Sterling like I'm supposed to?

"Here." Adam holds up his hands, and I throw him the ball. And then I pick up my violin again and . . . shove it against the wall. I fling my backpack next to it and run onto the court.

Our gym has shiny floors that make that squeaky sound if your sneakers are new. But we hardly ever get to play basketball in it. During recess we go outside if it isn't raining. With so many kids crammed on the blacktop, there's barely any room for a game. When there's indoor recess, we have to stay in our classrooms and play board games or talk quietly. In gym class we do other stuff, like climbing ropes and playing pickleball. I thought pickleball was a joke. But it's a real sport, like squash and my grandpa's favorite: cricket. I don't understand why they name sports after gross foods and insects.

Right now we have the full court all to ourselves. We get to use two regulation-height hoops that aren't bent. And Adam found a good indoor ball with lots of grip.

We play three-on-three, and I make a

few slick dribble moves and a couple of long-range jump shots. Then we play a game of H-O-R-S-E, and I come in second.

"You're trying out for our team, right?" Adam says when the early bell rings. We walk back to where my stuff is piled on the ground. Like most of the boys in my class, Adam's a lot taller than me. Lately he sways from side to side when he walks, like some of the fifth graders do.

"I already did." I think back to the tryouts we had in the summer, when I played terribly. Adam and Blake went to the gold team, and I was placed in the D league.

"Yeah. But you choked."

I pause. What if I don't make the team *again*? I hadn't considered that before.

"Maybe," I finally say. I don't mention that I've been planning on it all along.

"If you just practice with us in the mornings you'll make it. You're good enough."

Adam thinks I belong on the gold team too! I hide a smile and act cool.

"Okay," I say. "Promise you won't tell my mom. She'll kill me if she finds out I'm skipping orchestra."

"I won't." Adam puts his hand up and gives me the peace sign. "Scout's honor."

"That's not the Scout sign. I was a Cub Scout," Blake says. "It's this." He throws up a fake gang sign.

"No, it's this." Adam punches Blake in the shoulder, and then they start wrestling in the hall.

I *really* want to be on their team.

I walk the long way around the school to my classroom. That way I avoid passing the music room and bumping into Ms. Sterling. But this was a million times better than practicing the violin. I'll figure out an excuse about why I can't come for the next few weeks. And then I'll practice violin extra hard after tryouts to make up for it. Promise.

6

I was destroying the other team in NBA 2K when my mom called me upstairs this afternoon.

"You can play video games with Jamal Mamoo later. I need you to do other things right now," she said.

"Mamoo's coming? Today?" Mama's younger brother Jamal Mamoo has a beard and a job and everything, but he doesn't act like a grown-up. When he comes over, he hangs out with me in the basement or plays outside, instead of sitting with the adults. He taught me my killer serve in Ping-Pong. He shows me the funniest videos ever on YouTube. And he has the wackiest laugh, which makes everyone around him crack up, even if they didn't hear the joke.

"He's having dinner with us. I need you to help Zara empty the dishwasher, sweep the kitchen, and practice violin," Mama said. "Are you practicing? I haven't heard you in a while."

"Yeah," I mumbled. I made a mental note: Practice violin today so that wouldn't be a lie.

I did everything she asked without any complaining, thinking about all the fun I'd have later. Except now that mamoo is finally here, everyone else is hogging him.

Zara is perched on the armrest of Jamal Mamoo's chair, asking a million questions.

"Oh my God! Where are you going to meet her? What's her name? Where's she from? Do you have a picture?" She barely stops to breathe.

"Relax, Zara." Mamoo laughs. "A friend of Ammi's suggested I meet her. And I agreed. That's all. Don't start planning the wedding."

I can't believe it. I cleaned my room for *this*? Jamal Mamoo of all people is talking about *marriage*? He's the guy who ignores everyone's questions about marriage. He always rolls his eyes when Naano talks about finding him a "nice girl from good family." Or he says things like, "I'll get hitched when Zayd does."

"You sound like the cheesy younger brother

from *Dil Nahi Chahta*," I finally blurt out when I can't take it anymore. That guy is always meeting girls who never like him. It isn't a compliment.

"What did you say?" Jamal Mamoo gets up and stands over me. His crosses his arms and bugs out his eyes.

"Nothing," I say, shrinking into the couch.

"Really? Because I heard you." Jamal Mamoo tackles me and starts to tickle me.

"Stop! I'm going to pee!" I scream. I mean it. If he doesn't stop, I'm going to wet myself.

"Knock it off," Mama orders with a laugh. "I just steam cleaned."

Jamal Mamoo lets me go, and I'm panting and sweating now.

"I can't believe you're talking about marriage," I mumble.

"I can't believe how bony you are, Skeletor.

It hurts my fingers. Have you even hit sixty pounds yet, or what?"

Skeletor is mamoo's nickname for me because I'm skinny, and because he's a radiographer. I used to think that meant he worked at a radio station. But he actually takes pictures of people's insides with X-rays and other machines. He teases me and says that I look like the skeleton images he sees on the screen all day.

"Almost. I'm fifty-six pounds," I say.

"I wish he'd gain some weight," Mama says.

I hate it when people talk about me like I'm not even there.

"Some Cheetos might help," I suggest. Mama always says junk food makes you gain weight. But now she reads this nutrition blog that lists foods you should never buy your kids. And Cheetos were on it.

Jamal Mamoo lets out his wacky laugh.

"Your mom isn't buying you Cheetos!" he says. "But I'll make you a deal. You hit sixty pounds by the end of next month, and I'll get you an awesome prize."

"A new basketball hoop!" I shout.

"Uh. No. Think smaller."

"A signed Wall jersey?"

"Smaller. Like maybe a jumbo box of Cheetos." Jamal Mamoo laughs again while Mama starts to protest. "I'm kidding. I'll think about it. But you got to eat more and put on some pounds."

"Deal." We shake on it and then have a thumb war, which I lose like always. And then we play three games of NBA 2K, and I win two of them.

When I go up to my room at bedtime, I see the still-empty food journal sitting on my bedside table. I think about Jamal Mamoo's offer and flip it open to write in it for the very first time. If writing in this thing can do anything to help me put on some weight, I'm game.

DATE/TIME: 10/20, 8:47 p.m.

WHAT I ATE:

Almost all of the veggie burger Baba made (pretty good, but beef is better)

A slice of cheddar cheese, ketchup, and spicy barbecue sauce on the bun (whole wheat, not as good as sesame buns)

A handful of sweet potato fries (good, dipped in spicy barbecue sauce)

Spicy barbecue sauce

A few bites of salad (just for you, Mama!)

2 slices of the blueberry-peach pie Jamal Mamoo brought (now THAT'S what I'm talking about!)

HOW I FEEL: Super full, but a lot heavier already. I'm so getting that prize!

7

"Hey, Zayd!" Adam gets dropped off at school at the same time as me. A jolt of guilt hits me as I get out of my mom's car. She thinks I'm going to orchestra practice, even though I haven't been there in two weeks. But the feeling disappears as I follow Adam into the gym.

"My birthday's going to be at the trampoline place," Adam says. We peel off our jackets and pile our stuff by the door.

"My cousin had his party there. It was so fun."

"Did you do the basketball trampoline? You can jam the ball and everything."

"Yeah! It's awesome!" I say. "I did a three-sixty dunk and then fell on my face. But it didn't hurt."

"But you're always falling down," Adam reminds me.

"True."

Baba says I get knocked over easily because I'm so light. He also tells me I need to grow stronger and gain muscle. I've been eating as much as I can. I do push-ups and sit-ups and run sprints during basketball practice. What else am I supposed to do?

"Sorry I'm late. I turned off my alarm." Blake walks in wearing cool new sneakers with the Maryland flag design printed right on them. They are squeaking as he walks on the gym floor. I look down at my old shoes. They're dirty and worn out. But they still fit me, and there's no way I'm getting new ones until my feet grow. But I can't seem to make that happen any faster either.

"Where is everyone?" Adam looks at the clock. "Maybe Cody and Zane aren't coming today."

Adam acts like the coach of our morning practices, but no one seems to mind. He's always been someone that people listen to. Some might say bossy. But we've been best friends since first grade, and it's never bothered me.

"What should we do while we wait?" Adam asks. It's only been two weeks, but the extra practices are making a difference. I wonder if Coach Wheeler has noticed during my own team's practices.

"Let's do the halftime challenge like they do at Wizards games," Blake suggests. "See if you can make a layup, free throw, and three-pointer in sixty seconds."

"What does the winner get?" I ask.

"A signed ball or tickets to box seats or something."

"No, I mean right now," I say.

Blake searches through his pockets.

"How about a watermelon Jolly Rancher?"

"It's on."

Blake goes first while I keep time. He makes an easy layup. Then he's stuck at the free throw line forever.

"Come on, Blake!" Adam shouts.

"Time's up!" I yell. Blake falls to the ground and lies there like he's dead.

I go next. I miss the layup the first time and then get the next one in. I run to grab the ball, double back to the free throw line. The shot goes in with a satisfying

SWISH.

"Nice!" Adam is looking at his watch. "Fourteen seconds to go. You can do this!"

I race to the three-point line with the ball in my hands. I bounce it a couple of times and then release the ball.

"ZAYD!" I hear a voice that sounds familiar yell out my name from behind me.

I whip my head around. And then I freeze.

Standing there, in the doorway to the gym, is my *mother*. She's holding my violin case. Her face is set in stone. And I miss the shot by a mile.

8

"Hi, Mama." I walk over to her like there's nothing strange at all about her finding me hanging out in the gym. Maybe she'll think I only came in here *because* I forgot my violin and had nothing else to do before school. Yeah! That's it! I was only shooting hoops because I had *no other choice*.

"What are you doing here?" she asks.

"I, um, well, I forgot my violin. Right? So I came here to shoot around until school starts." I drop my head and kick the floor as I speak.

"Oh, I see. You forgot your violin."

She's falling for this? I look up in surprise.

"For TWO WHOLE WEEKS?" Mama explodes. "I went to look for you in the music room. And I saw Ms. Sterling. And guess what she said?"

I don't say anything. But I find a tiny hole near the tip of my shoe.

"Answer me. What do you think she said?" Mama presses.

"That she didn't like my idea. To get me a seat belt for the next concert?" I try to joke. I sneak a glance at Mama now. She's almost as purple as the scarf around her neck. And she isn't smiling.

"No, Zayd. Let me think. She said something about . . . what was it? Oh, yeah. How you told her you can't come to morning practice anymore because your parents CAN'T BRING YOU!"

I'm pretty sure I'm still breathing, but I don't move.

"Zayd! Are you listening? Look at me!"

I meet Mama's eyes. If they could shoot laser beams, I would be dust right now.

"Sorry, Mama," I mumble.

"That's it? That's all you have to say? I get ready at the crack of dawn to bring you here in the mornings. I use my hard-earned money to pay for your lessons. And you LIE to me and to your teacher and come in here to BOUNCE A BALL around?"

I nod my head. The way she puts it, it does sound like a bad idea.

"And how long were you planning to keep this up?"

"Um . . . I don't know. Maybe until tryouts?"

Mama shakes her head slowly. It looks like someone let all the air out of her. All of a sudden I feel like a basketball has whacked me in the stomach. I need to sit down.

"Mama, ever since I fell off the stage, Ms. Sterling's been acting weird. During class she's always telling me to—"

"Don't you dare," Mama cuts me off. "This isn't about her. You need to own this, Zayd." She looks around as the early bell rings.

Adam and Blake are on the other side of the gym, quietly dribbling and pretending not to listen. I'm pretty sure they can hear us.

"Sorry," I mutter again. I take the violin from my mother and go pick up my backpack and jacket.

"We'll discuss this later at home," Mama says. As Adam passes us, she gives him a stern stare. Mama usually hugs Adam whenever she sees him. But I guess he's an accomplice right now.

"Okay," I agree.

As she leaves, Adam gives me a sympathetic look. Blake hands me the watermelon Jolly Rancher. But I can't eat it right now. I didn't win the contest. And I feel like I lost a whole lot. I just don't know exactly what yet.

9

I'd be lying if I said I'm not a little scared to go home. I walk slowly from the bus stop to my house and ring the doorbell since I forgot my key. Phew. Zara opens the door.

"Hey," she says. She's still turned around, watching the TV in the other room.

"Where's Mama?"

"Store. I made kettle corn," Zara offers. She holds out a bowl of the sweet-and-salty popcorn.

"I'm not hungry." I didn't finish my lunch, but I can't eat right now. My stomach twists into knots every time I think about what happened this morning.

"Okay." Zara walks back to the family room and settles onto the sofa.

I head up to my room. The food journal is sitting on my desk, staring at me. I haven't touched it again since my first entry. I remember my mom's face at school and decide it's a good time to listen to her. So I open it up and write:

DATE/TIME: 10/26, 3:27 p.m.

WHAT I ATE:

Half a turkey sandwich (minus the crust)

17 goldfish crackers, cheddar flavor

6 bites of my apple

Watermelon Jolly Rancher

HOW I FEEL: Like someone is dribbling a ball on my insides.

Then I do my homework, lie on my bed, and look at an old issue of *Sports Illustrated Kids* that Blake gave me. It's got an amazing photo of John Wall making a fadeaway jumper.

"ZAYD!" I hear my father calling me. So I drag myself off the bed and go downstairs.

"Have a seat," my dad says, pointing to the dining table. Mama is back and already sitting there. We never use the dining table except for parties, making posters for school projects, and family meetings. I feel my heart pounding in my throat.

I decide to apologize before he gets going.

"Baba, I . . ."

"Hold on." Baba stops me as Zara walks into the room. She's carrying a book and wearing headphones. And she's pretending that she only happened to come into the room we never use. But we all know she's spying.

"Zara, can you excuse us, please?"

"Yeah, sure," Zara says. She gives me a look and mouths "You're dead!" on her way out.

Baba frowns, gives me a long stare, and then speaks.

"Your mother told me what happened. We're disappointed in you for lying to us. And to your teacher."

"Baba, I . . ." I start to apologize again.

"I'm not done. You committed to playing the violin. We paid to rent it. And we pay for you to be in the orchestra. It's a lot of money, time, and effort," Baba continues. Mama just nods her head.

I nod my head too.

"We know you like basketball. We've supported you. But now you lose it."

"What?" I gasp.

"You won't be playing any basketball for the next two weeks. And then we'll see after that."

"But I'm on a team!" I protest.

"You were in an orchestra, too, and you didn't worry about that. Your team will manage without you."

I feel my heart sink into my stomach as I realize tryouts are in less than two weeks.

"What about tryouts? I have to go to tryouts or I won't be able to move up to the gold team!" I know I should stop arguing, but I can't help it.

"You need to practice violin, to make up for the past two weeks. And you need to earn back our trust. Basketball is the least of your concerns right now."

I sit there, stunned.

"Do you understand me?" Baba continues. "No watching basketball either. Or reading about it. Or talking about it. I don't want to see that you are even thinking about basketball. Got it?"

I nod my head again and blink back tears. I can't believe I'm going to miss my chance to move out of the D league. Last time I lied to my parents, it wasn't on purpose. It kind of just happened. But right now I'm lying for real. Because I don't know how I'm not going to think about basketball. It's what I do more than anything else.

10

Even though Jamal Mamoo is meeting a girl to see if they might want to get married, we're all going. That means my family, Naano and Nana Abu, and mamoo have to drive all the way from Maryland to Virginia to this girl's house. And it means that I have to dress up nice to impress these people.

"That's what family's for," Baba declares when I grumble about wearing my button-down shirt with black pants. It's the same outfit I wear for orchestra concerts. And I don't need any reminders about that. My life has been all violin and no basketball for the past week.

"Try harder!" Mama orders while I shove my foot into one of the dress shoes that I found in a corner of the hall closet after searching everywhere. My heel won't go in all the way.

"When did you outgrow these?" she wonders aloud.

"I thought you wanted me to grow," I reply. Mama sighs. But Jamal Mamoo chuckles as I grab my sneakers.

"You wearing those, Skeletor? They're pretty beat up."

"I know. But they fit."

"How about that for your prize when you hit sixty pounds?" Jamal Mamoo suggests. "Some new kicks."

"Jordans?" I whisper so my parents don't hear me. I've wanted a pair of Air Jordans since forever, but my parents think they're way too expensive. Plus, I'm still being punished, and this conversation is technically about basketball.

"Yeah, sure," he says.

"Really?" I can't believe it.

"Come on, come on! We're going to be late." Baba rolls his eyes when he sees my shoes but doesn't say anything. We stumble out the door with arms full of gifts for the strangers: cake, flowers, a bunch of Pakistani sweets, and a fruit basket.

When we get there, an older auntie in a pink shalwar kameez and a scarf on her hair opens the door with a smile. A gray-haired uncle is standing behind her.

"Asalaamualaikum! Please, please, come in," they say.

We file into the house and take off our shoes. At that moment I see that one of my dressy black socks has a giant hole, and my big toe is completely

sticking out. It must have ripped when I was shoving my foot into the tight shoe. I nudge Jamal Mamoo, and we both start to giggle.

"Shhhh!" Mama scolds as we make our way to a formal living room. There are sofas with carved wooden arms along the walls. Nana Abu settles into one of the sofas and smiles at everyone. But Naano looks like she is sitting on a pile of rocks and keeps squirming. I try to hide my naked toe under my other foot.

After a while, the auntie serves us drinks on a tray. I take a little napkin and manage not to spill as I lift up a soda, ignoring Mama's raised eyebrow. Of course soda is on the list of junk foods never to let your kids have.

And then the girl walks into the room. I feel bad for her because we all stare at her like she's an alien wearing a blue shalwar kameez. But she acts like she doesn't notice and smiles at all of us. She says salaam and "it's nice to meet you" in perfect Urdu. Then she takes a seat near Naano, who I can tell likes her already.

"This is Nadia," her mother says proudly.

I sneak a peek at Jamal Mamoo, who is

sitting next to me. He's turning red and acting like he's trying to look and *not* look at Nadia at the same time.

"It's nice to meet you, Nadia," Mama says. And then there's nothing but awkward silence.

"Nadia is finishing up nursing school," her father finally says after clearing his throat.

"Jamal is a radiographer." Nana Abu smiles. "That's nice, mashallah. They are both in the health field."

And then everyone is quiet again.

I give Jamal Mamoo a little nudge with my elbow. It means, "Dude, say something." But my loud, funny uncle has turned into this silent, sweaty, nervous guy. Next I try to poke mamoo with my big toe—the one that's sticking out. But he doesn't even crack a smile. In Naano's drama, the main character is always charming and funny when he meets girls. But mamoo is the total opposite.

"So, Nadia . . . um . . . auntie," I finally pipe up. "Do you like sports?"

"I do, Zayd," she says brightly. I'm surprised she knows my name. "Football and basketball most. What about you?"

"Yeah. Basketball most. Are you a Wizards fan?" I hold my breath. She could be the perfect wife. For Jamal Mamoo, I mean.

"I'm from Chicago. Bulls all the way."

"Oh." My hope fizzles.

But Jamal Mamoo takes my lead. "Cubs or White Sox?"

"Cubbies all the way!" she says.

As the two of them start talking about stadiums and good restaurants, the rest of us slowly leave the room. Zara and I end up watching a cartoon movie in the den. The grown-ups chat in the dining room. Naano is putting on a show and is telling her favorite jokes. I hear laughing and the sound of teacups clinking. And I remember the Jordans and help myself to an extra-big slice of cake from the table.

As we leave, Jamal Mamoo stops me in the hall and gives me a friendly shove.

"Hey, Skeletor. Thanks for jumping in. That was a good call."

"No problem," I say. "I got you."

As I shove mamoo back, I decide that Baba was right about that whole "that's what family's for" thing after all.

11

Ever since I've been grounded, Zara's been rubbing it in my face.

"Can you believe Wall and Beal both got double-doubles last night? Wall scored twenty-three points in the second half."

I make a face at her over my cereal.

"Oh, yeah. You couldn't watch the game." She fakes a sad face. "Want to shoot around?"

Now I stick my tongue out, covered in mushed oat flakes and milk.

"Oh, man, that's right. You can't. How about we play some 2K?"

"YOU'RE NOT FUNNY, ZARA!" I shout, glad when little drops of cereal milk spray out of my mouth in her direction.

"Zayd! Don't yell at your sister," Mama says as she walks into the kitchen. "I need you to practice violin, then get ready. I'm dropping you guys off at Naano's."

"Why?" I ask.

"Baba and I are going to the mosque to plan the fund-raiser. Would you rather come? I don't think kids will be there."

"I want to go to Naano's," I say. I drag myself to the living room and pick up my violin. I wonder if everyone else in the house is sick of hearing me play "Song for Christine" over and over. I imagine my parents wearing earplugs and secretly wishing I was playing basketball instead. It makes me feel a little better about my punishment. I play as loudly as I can.

When we arrive at my grandparents' house, Naano opens the door in her fuzzy slippers.

"Zayd. My skinny mouse. Let's eat something. What you want? Zara, come."

"I'm good, Naano. I promise I already ate," I say as I walk into the family room, where the TV is on, like usual. But instead of dramas or Pakistani news or cricket, Nana Abu is watching a game I've never seen before.

"What is this, Nana Abu?" I ask.

"Kabaddi," he says.

"Ka-buddy?"

"No, kabaddi," he repeats.

"That's what I said. What are they doing?"

"I played this game when I was a boy. This is the world cup." Nana Abu sounds proud. But he doesn't explain how the game works, so I try to figure it out.

The teams are on opposite sides of a court. One person from each team tries to tag a player on the other team. And even though it sounds like a joke, the defenders all *hold hands* and hop around. And then the tagger, who the announcer is calling a "raider," starts to bob and weave, like a boxer. Sometimes the chain breaks and the other team grabs him and throws him to the ground. It looks confusing, like tag and wrestling and ring-around-the-rosie at the same time.

"When I was a boy, in my village, we would wear nothing but our chaddis and grease our bodies with oil so the other team couldn't

grab us," Nana Abu explains with a gleam in
his eye.

"Were you on a team?" I ask.

"Not a team like yours," he says. "We made
our own teams. But, oh, it was so much fun."

"I can't play on my team anymore," I say.
"My parents won't let me."

"That's because he lied," Zara volunteers.

"Why you tell lie?" Naano asks. "Serves you right."

But Nana Abu gives me a gentle smile.

"I'll teach you a new game," he says.

"Ka-buddy?" I ask, worried. The last thing I need to do is wrestle my slicked-up grandfather wearing nothing but giant underwear.

"No. This game is called carom. Come with me."

Nana Abu shuffles over to the closet and pulls out a large square wooden board with pockets in the corners. He finds a box with disk pieces in it. Zara and I help him lay the board flat on a small side table and sprinkle powder on it. The disks slide around on the smooth board like an air hockey table, without the air.

Nana Abu arranges the pieces in the middle of the board. He points to a bigger disk. "This is the striker. This is the queen," he says, motioning to a red piece. "That goes in last."

"It's so cute," Zara says. "Like a tiny pool table."

She's right. Except instead of a pool stick, in carom you use your fingers to flick the striker toward the pieces you want to get into the pockets.

We spend the afternoon challenging Nana Abu and losing to him each time. But I get the hang of it faster than Zara and easily beat her.

"I can't get the pieces in!" Zara whines. She isn't used to not being the best at something.

I, on the other hand, do know what that's like. So for the next hour it feels great to cream her at carom, my new second-favorite game. And I make sure to rub it in, just a little. Okay, a lot.

12

"Great job, Zayd." Ms. Sterling doesn't hide the surprise in her voice. "I can tell you've been practicing."

"Thanks," I mutter. I have to admit that I can tell I sound better too. But it doesn't make me like playing the violin any more. I know my friends are still playing basketball on the other side of the school. And that's where I want to be.

"You know, Zayd," Ms. Sterling continues, as if she is reading my mind. "Many famous athletes are musicians. It's a great way to relax."

"Really?" I ask. "Like who?"

"Well, Shaquille O'Neal recorded music for starters," she says.

"I guess so." I pack up my instrument and don't tell her Shaquille O'Neal recorded *rap* music. I'd love to do that too.

Ms. Sterling makes me think of basketball again, and for a moment I hope we can play at recess. Until I remember my punishment. No basketball for a few more days. Plus it was raining this morning, so we'll probably be stuck inside anyway. It's been raining a lot this week, and we've had indoor recess every day. It's making everyone grumpy.

We've been playing cards in our classroom since we can't go outside. Adam taught Blake and me how to play Egyptian War. It's like regular War, except you throw down your cards really fast, you can play with more than one other person, and you have to slap the cards whenever there are two of the same. If you slap the cards first, you get the whole pile. Whoever gets all the cards wins.

"You didn't shuffle," Adam complains. It's recess, and we're in the classroom with our cards.

"I did too. You saw me," I argue.

"You have all the jacks. No fair."

We throw our cards down so fast it's almost a blur. But then I spot two sevens.

THWACK!

Adam's hand slaps the table, and my hand hits the top of his.

"Ha! Got it!" He grins.

We start throwing cards down again, and this time I see two queens.

THWACK!

I get there first, but Blake tries to slide his hand underneath and jabs me with his fingernail.

"OW!" I howl.

"SHHH. Boys, keep it down," Mrs. Neal orders.

"Nasty! Cut your nails! They're disgusting," I grumble.

Blake inspects his nails.

"Doesn't bother me." He shrugs.

"Yeah, but remember when half of Cody's nail ripped off during basketball practice?" Adam warns him. "You should cut them."

"Yeah," I agree. I rub my hand and make sure he didn't draw blood.

"When can you play with us again?" Adam asks me. "Isn't your punishment over?"

"Almost," I say. "But I'm back in orchestra in the mornings anyway."

"Wait. You're still coming to tryouts, though, right?" Adam looks worried.

"I'm still grounded then."

"No way! That sucks." Adam frowns.

"I would die if I couldn't play basketball for so long," Blake adds.

"Yeah."

"Maybe you can get Coach to let you try out later." Adam is trying to encourage me, like usual.

"I don't know. Coach might be mad at me already." Mama e-mailed Coach Wheeler to say I wasn't going to be at practice or games for the two weeks I'm being grounded. I wonder what will happen when I go back. Maybe he'll make me sit on the bench.

"Well, he can't kick you out of the D league," Blake chimes in. "Can he?"

"Dude, you're not helping." Adam punches Blake in the shoulder. "You'll figure it out, Zayd, don't worry."

I can't help but worry, and I think about missing tryouts all day. Mrs. Carson says I'm "distracted" during science, when she calls on me and I'm not paying attention. But while she goes on and on about genetics and earlobes, my stomach starts to hurt. This time it's really hurting, like someone is wringing out my insides like a sponge.

I raise my hand.

"Can I go to the nurse?" I ask.

13

"Zayd, I haven't seen you in a while," Mrs. Diallo says when I walk into the small health room by the office. "What's the matter?"

"My stomach hurts. Can I lie down?"

"Sure, honey. Do you need me to call your mom?"

"Okay," I moan. I crawl onto the little cot by the door. It smells like the tub of Clorox wipes sitting on the table next to it.

"Mrs. Saleem?" I hear Mrs. Diallo speaking into the phone. "I have Zayd at the nurse's station. He's complaining of stomach pain. Oh, let me ask."

Mrs. Diallo turns to me. "Zayd? Mom is asking if you need to use the bathroom?"

"Um. No," I say. I feel my face grow hot. Isn't that *personal*?

"He says no. Oh, I see. Okay. I'll let him know. Thanks," Mrs. Diallo continues into the phone.

"Is she coming?" I ask.

"She says someone will come pick you up."

"Okay." I close my eyes, trying to shut the pain out. I play the song we were practicing in violin in my head and lie there, curled up in a ball.

The next thing I know, I feel a gentle shaking. I open my eyes to see Jamal Mamoo standing over me in light blue scrubs. I must have fallen asleep.

"Salaams, Skeletor," he says.

"Salaams," I say, rubbing my eyes.

"How you feeling?"

"Better. My . . ." I start to say that my stomach isn't hurting anymore. But Jamal Mamoo shakes his head and winks at me. So I stop talking.

"Where do I sign him out?" he turns and asks Mrs. Diallo in his most charming voice.

"Next door, in the main office. Feel better, Zayd," she says.

"Thanks." I try to sound more miserable than I feel.

We walk out to the parking lot after I go collect my backpack, lunch bag, and violin from my cubby. I feel guilty because everyone looks sorry for me, and I'm totally fine. My stomach doesn't hurt a bit. It's like nothing ever happened. Plus it's finally stopped raining, and the sun is starting to peek out.

"But, Mamoo, I'm okay now," I whisper, even though we've left the building and are almost at his car. "I can go back to class."

"I had to drive all the way out here. And if I'm missing work, you're skipping the rest of the day. Deal?"

"Deal," I agree. "Where are we going?"

"Hungry?" he asks.

"Kind of."

"Let's get some chicken."

14

We pull up in front of a place called Crisp & Juicy.

"Don't tell Naano, but this is the best chicken in town. You like plantains and yucca?" Mamoo doesn't wait for me to answer and orders a family platter, for the two of us.

"So, what's going on with you?" he asks

after he carries the tray to a table in the corner. Mamoo tears the chicken apart and puts a huge piece in front of me. "This should help put some meat on you. Try this sauce."

I take a bite of the chicken. Like the restaurant's name, it's crisp and juicy, and delicious.

"What happened to you today? Did you have a test? Someone mean to you?"

"No."

"Well, then, what's going on with you?"

"Nothing."

"What were you thinking about when your stomach started hurting?"

"Tryouts. I've been dying to be on the gold team. And now I'm going to miss my chance since I can't go. I haven't played any basketball for nine days, when I should have been practicing extra hard. I've missed all the

Wizards games on TV. And I can't even play 2K." Everything pours out.

"Oh, I see." Jamal Mamoo's forehead wrinkles. "Do you have a cough?"

"No."

"Body aches?"

"No."

"Do you drool when you sleep?"

"Maybe a little."

"I think I know what you are suffering from."

"What?" I ask.

"*Agonia hoopidynia.* Sounds like a bad case." Jamal Mamoo shakes his head sadly.

"WHAT?"

"*Hoopidynia.* Haven't you heard of it?"

"Oh my God. Is it serious?"

"I think you'll survive. But you'll need treatment."

"Does it hurt?" I feel my stomach tighten again.

"As bad as when I destroy you in one on one."

I finally realize he's teasing me. HOOP-idynia. Corny.

"Very funny, Mamoo. You freaked me out!"

Mamoo grins, then gets serious.

"Listen, Zayd. You need to stand up for yourself. Tell your parents how much these tryouts and this team mean to you. Maybe they'll understand why you did such a boneheaded thing."

"But Mama wants me to play violin more than basketball. I've been playing so much violin it's ridiculous. I want to quit and focus on basketball."

I've never said that before, but it's true.

"I get it. You need to make them understand what *you* want. For yourself."

"Have you ever tried to change my mom's mind about anything?" I ask.

"Good point." Mamoo smiles. "Just be strong."

I chew for a minute and think about what he said. Then I say what else is on my mind.

"What about you? *You're* not standing up for yourself."

"Excuse me?" Mamoo raises his eyebrows.

"You're letting everyone make you get married."

Mamoo laughs so loudly the people at the other tables all look at us. One lady even starts to giggle even though she doesn't know why.

"Nice try, Skeletor. It's not that. I'm just realizing that it might finally be the right time to find someone. You don't want me to be alone forever, do you?"

"I guess not."

"Look, there's a difference between letting your family guide you and letting them stop you from following your true passion. Get it?"

I suddenly think about the poor guy in *Dil Nahi Chahta* trying to make movies while his parents freak out about medical school. I nod my head. And I decide that I hope he gets to make his movies, even if they look like ones I'd never want to watch.

"I have faith you can convince your parents," mamoo says as he pulls a leg off the chicken and drops it on my plate. "And that you'll eat more chicken. I can't finish this platter by myself."

15

At night, before bed, I take a deep breath and march into the family room. Mama and Baba are sitting on the sofa with their laptops. I make sure Mama isn't paying bills, since that makes her cranky. She's online, looking at someone's wedding photos. That's a good sign.

"Mama? Baba?" I say.

"Hey, hon. What's up?" Mama's still looking at the screen. I would get in trouble for doing that.

"You tell me that I should always be honest with you, right?" I start.

"Of course," Mama says. She's giving me her full attention now. I imagine serious violin music playing in the background and try to push it out of my head.

"I know I should have told you I was skipping violin. But the honest truth is, I don't want to play it anymore."

"What do you mean?" Mama starts to shake her head. "You've been playing for more than a year now. And you're good at it!"

"But I don't like it. I don't like practicing it. I don't like my lessons. I don't like being in the orchestra. I don't even like the way the violin *sounds*."

"That's absurd," Mama snorts. "How can you not like the way a violin sounds? It's beautiful."

"Maybe to you," I continue. "But I like hip-hop."

Mama looks crushed.

"But you have so much potential," she says. "You'll learn to appreciate it."

"I don't want to. I want to play basketball. And be on the gold team. And I skipped violin because I wanted to have a better chance at tryouts."

"But, Zayd, you're so . . ." Baba stops himself and looks a little embarrassed.

I wait for him to finish.

"The other kids have a real size advantage over you. Don't you think it makes more sense for you to . . . um . . . maybe focus on a different sport?"

"Like what?"

"Like tennis. Or swimming. You were always a good swimmer."

"I'm good at basketball, too. I've gotten a lot better than I was. At least I *was* getting better. Before you made me stop."

Mama and Baba look at each other.

"Plus all my friends play basketball," I add.

"Well, if all your friends—" Baba starts.

"I promise I would *not* jump off a cliff," I interrupt.

Baba smiles.

"I was going to say that if all your friends play, I can see why you want to also. But don't jump off a cliff, either."

"Can I please, PLEASE go to tryouts this weekend? My two weeks are almost up. I can make up the extra days later? Please?"

"We appreciate you being honest with us,"

Mama says. "Let your dad and me talk about it."

I start to feel lighter.

"But you know that it's good to stick with something you start," she adds. "And you've already invested time and energy learning to play the violin."

"Zara got to quit tap dance," I mumble. "And softball. And kung fu."

"Okay, Zayd. It's not a competition with Zara." Mama picks up her laptop again, but her eyes are smiling. "Besides, playing the violin is different. It helps develop your brain. We just want to help you grow."

I don't say that it won't help me grow heavier or taller. And that's the only kind of growing I'm really interested in right now.

"Just think seriously about this decision, and we will too," Mama says. "Okay?"

"Okay, I will."

Even though she still needs to think about it, I don't. I should have told them what I felt weeks ago. Ever since the day I fell off that stage I knew it was meant to be my grand finale. Like mamoo said, I need to follow my true passion.

16

"Gentlemen, are we looking up information for our research projects or goofing around?"

Mrs. Griffin is glaring at us over her reading glasses from the checkout desk in the media center.

"Looking up information," Adam says, as

he pokes me under the table. We're sitting at the computers to do research for our role-models project.

"Check this out!" Adam clicks on a YouTube video called "Kevin Durant's Greatest Moments." There are three guys in regular clothes talking about Durant and imitating his signature moves on a court. And they name each one something goofy like the Matrix.

"He's amazing," Adam sighs. "And you know . . ."

"I *know*. Your cousin went to high school with him at Montrose Christian. You told me a thousand times."

"You're just jealous."

"It wasn't *you*, was it?"

"Still. My cousin knows him. And I know my cousin. So it's like I know him."

"BOYS!" Mrs. Griffin sneaks up behind us,

and we both jump. "That does *not* look like research!"

"Yes it is." Adam turns to a page in his notebook and points to the title. "It's research, promise. Look. I picked Kevin Durant as my role model."

Mrs. Griffin lets out a big sigh. "A football player? That's the best you could come up with?"

"Basketball. And he *is* the best," Adam argues. "He's tall *and* he can shoot."

"Well, I hope you can find other reasons why he is a true role model. What about you, Zayd? Who do you have?"

"John Wall."

"Let me guess, another athlete?"

"Not just another athlete. He's MVP of the Wizards. He leads the league in assists. And he—"

"Okay, okay." Mrs. Griffin frowns. "I get the idea. But you need to find at least two reasons to admire these individuals outside of sports."

Adam and I look at each other. Mrs. Griffin is taking all the fun out of this project.

"And I expect you to use the Internet to look up articles, boys. No more videos."

"Okay," we both say.

I spend the next half hour trying to find out other stuff about John Wall besides his shooting average. And I'm surprised how much there is.

"John Wall's awesome," I say.

"Not as awesome as KD," Adam argues.

"I'm not talking about basketball. He won a Community Assist Award for doing all this cool stuff."

"Like what?"

"Helping homeless kids, and building

playgrounds and things." I point to the article on the screen. "And I touched him," I add.

"I know. You told me a thousand times."

Adam is just getting back at me for not acting impressed enough about Durant and his cousin. But I really did touch John Wall. It was when Jamal Mamoo took me to a Wizards game last year for my birthday, up in the highest section of the arena. Right before halftime we went down to the spot where the players pass by to go to the locker room.

I got to high-five most of the team, and even though I missed John Wall, I touched his arm as he walked by. His sweat absorbed into my skin. I told Mamoo I was never going to wash that hand again. He made me wash it ten minutes later when he bought me a hot dog. But it was still awesome. I *touched* John Wall!

Adam checks to make sure Mrs. Griffin

isn't looking and clicks on a website called Land of Basketball, where you can compare stats of players side by side.

"KD is better than Wall. No comparison. And he helps kids too," he gloats. "Look."

Durant has beaten Wall in every single category except for steals and assists.

I just shrug since I can't argue with the numbers. But Wall is still my favorite player. And he's going to be my role model, whether Mrs. Griffin likes it or not. Because you're supposed to learn something from a role model, right? And John Wall has taught me that sometimes you have to work extra hard to prove you're an all-star, even if others don't see it. And even if you're better than the team you're on. Plus, it's pretty cool that he likes to help people too.

17

"You need to man up," Zara sighs. "You can't fall down every time someone bumps into you."

"I'm not trying to," I grumble.

"Try to widen your stance a little, and press yourself into the ground," Jamal Mamoo suggests. "It'll make it harder for someone to knock you over."

"And you have to use your body more when you play," Zara adds. "Don't be afraid to be aggressive."

"I'm not afraid!" I want to shove her and show her how aggressive I can be. But I don't. Even though she's super annoying, Zara's trying to help for a change. Tryouts are in two days and I need all the practice I can get to make up for lost time. I'm just so happy that Mama and Baba agreed to let me try out. They said that they thought I had learned my lesson. And I don't even have to make up the last few days of my punishment.

"She's right, Zayd," Jamal Mamoo agrees. "You pass the ball too quickly when anyone presses you. You have to take it inside sometimes. Get into beast mode."

It's hard hearing everyone telling me what to do. I've been getting it from Coach, who was really tough on me when I went back to practice yesterday. Any time I missed a layup, he made me drop down and do ten extra push-ups. But I'm playing again, so I did it all without complaining.

"Here, try to get by me," Jamal Mamoo says. He passes me the ball.

I start to dribble, cut to my left, and then drive by him. He grabs me and picks me up, so I'm dangling in midair.

"No fair!" I yell while he laughs.

"Come in, you guys, and wash up for dinner!" Mama calls from the garage door.

I head inside and wash my hands, taking time to scrub all the black off, instead of just rinsing them.

"Zayd, come here for a minute." Mama pulls me into the family room before I go into the kitchen.

"I see how happy you are to be playing basketball again," she starts. "But I want you to remember why you were punished in the first place."

"I do."

"You know that you can always tell us what you want. Even if you think we won't like it, okay?"

"Okay."

"And I think it takes guts to say what you did about not wanting to play the violin the other night. Although I wish you would still play."

"Mama," I begin to protest. But Baba is standing behind her and signals for me to let her keep talking.

"I know, I know. I can't help that I do. But Mamoo reminded me how much I hated ballet when I was little and Naano made me take lessons."

"You did ballet?" I've never heard this before.

"For a little while. I used to cry about wearing those horribly itchy tights and that frilly pink tutu."

I imagine my mom in a tutu and fight back a smile.

"And I don't want to force you to do something you don't enjoy. Baba and I both want you to do what you love," Mama continues. "As long as you are always honest with us, Zayd. That's the most important thing. Understand?"

"Yeah."

"Okay, good. I'll tell Ms. Sterling that you're going to stop with the advanced orchestra. But will you still play during instrumental music, once a week? That way you can use the rental for the rest of the year."

"Sure," I say. That sounds fair enough. "I can do that."

"Great." Mama looks pleased.

"And, Mama, since we're being honest . . ."

"Yeah?"

"I wish you would cook normal food and let us eat junk again."

Baba gives me another signal that Mama can totally see this time: a double thumbs-up.

"Very funny, guys. That's not open for debate." Mama ruffles up my hair and gives me a hug. "Love you. Let's go eat."

"Love you too."

As we walk into the kitchen, it smells like we are at Naano's place instead of ours.

"Mmmm. What are we having?" Zara sniffs hard.

"Biryani," Naano says triumphantly. "And chapli kabob. I bring it."

"Yum." Baba grins.

"And for you, skinny mouse, mango lassi," Naano adds.

"But I don't like mango."

"Bakwas! Everyone likes mango," Naano

says before she realizes I'm kidding. Mangoes are my favorite fruit.

"*This* will make you fat and big," she says. We all know what she means. I've been eating so much lately. I'm still trying to get my new shoes from Mamoo. And I can use all the help I can get.

As I sip the sweet orange-colored milk shake, I look around the room. Nana Abu is piling a heap of biryani on his plate, and Mama is trying to squeeze some salad on the side. Baba is quizzing Zara on the periodic table of elements, and she is getting them all right. And Jamal Mamoo is buttering Naano up by telling her no future wife of his will ever cook as well as her.

After dinner I go upstairs and see my food journal by my bed. The other day Mama told me that she thinks my stomachaches happen when I'm worried about something, not because of an allergy or anything else. I think she's right. But they are happening less and less, which is good. The best part is she said I don't need to write in the journal anymore. But I flip it open anyway, just for fun, and enter in:

DATE/TIME: 11/9, 8:33 p.m.

WHAT I ATE:

A big pile of chicken biryani (Naano's masterpiece! Just the right amount of spicy)

1 1/2 chapli kabobs (if you pick out the tomatoes and onions, they are delicious)

Cucumber salad (chopped up cucumbers with salt and pepper on them that Naano took out for me, without adding yogurt to them. She's the best.)

A jumbo glass of mango lassi (which was amazing! Did I mention that Naano is the best?)

HOW I FEEL: Lucky

18

"Keanu! Pass!" I hold out my arms, and Keanu flings me the ball. I take a jumper and lose my balance. I'm falling. Again. But this time, as I hit the ground, I bounce and do a little somersault.

Keanu runs over and jumps on top of me,

and we bounce off the ground together. In a flash there's a huge pile of people on top of me.

"I can't breathe!" I shout. But I can't tell if it's because of the smelly socks in my face, or from laughing so hard.

"Watch this," Adam says after everyone rolls off me. He runs into the wall and does a half backflip into the middle of the trampoline.

No wonder Mama had to come inside and sign all these permission forms before Adam's party.

"Be careful, okay?" she warned. "You don't want to get hurt right before tryouts." So far three people have left the trampoline room limping. But there was no way I was going to sit out Adam's birthday party. And I survived without any twists or sprains.

"Time for cake, everyone," Mrs. Siegal announces.

We all crowd around Adam as he gets ready to blow out his candles. He looks around the room as we sing and then turns to me as he blows out his candles.

"You're going to do awesome at tryouts," he says. I squeeze by him to get a piece of cake. "You're going to make the team. I know it."

I don't ask if that's what he wished for. But I hope it is.

The next morning Mr. Siegal drives us to the middle school for tryouts. I try to ignore the mild churning in my stomach. I can't tell if it's the oatmeal Mama said would give me energy or my nerves. Maybe both.

When we walk into the gym, it's packed with kids.

"Why are there so many people here?" My voice is several pitches higher than usual. That has to be my nerves.

"This is fourth-, fifth-, and sixth-grade team tryouts. Don't worry," Adam says as we watch a kid who is almost six feet tall make an easy free throw.

Coach Wheeler blows the whistle and organizes us into groups. For the next hour he runs a bunch of drills. We start by running suicides back and forth across the gym. Then we do things like dribbling around cones and shooting from the free throw line and elbows. I make most of my shots and only flub my dribble once.

"You're playing like a boss," Adam says during water break. I hope he's right, because Coach Wheeler isn't giving away anything with his face.

Finally, we scrimmage. Somehow everything goes wrong. First, I botch a pass and turn the ball over. Then, on a fast break, I brick an easy layup. Worst of all I trip over my own feet while going for a steal and land on my face. OUCH!

I peel myself off the floor and avoid looking at Coach. I better do something to turn this around. And quick.

"Zayd!" Adam passes me the ball. I pump fake, and the defender takes the bait. I follow with a spin move and see the center coming to me. Before he gets to me, I step back into a fade-away jumper. Nothing but net! Adam gives me a high five. We would be awesome teammates.

On the next possession I steal the ball from a redheaded kid and lead my team down the court on a fast break. When I hit the free throw line, a defender jumps in my face. So I make a quick bounce pass to Adam, who finishes an easy layup. It's classic John Wall. I think he'd be proud.

I steal a look at Coach Wheeler and see a slight nod, as if he agrees with what I'm thinking. I'll take it. All I can do now is pray that I did enough to make the cut.

19

"I'm so full, but these noodles are so good," Zara says as she slurps chow mein off her plate.

I turn the disk in the middle of the table we're all seated around so I can reach what's left of the noodles. There is so much food spinning in front of me, it's dizzying. There's fried rice, chicken, shrimp, hot-and-sour soup and more.

We're at my grandparents' favorite Chinese restaurant, Good Fortune. It's also one of the only places Naano likes to go out to eat, besides IHOP. Most of the other places we've taken her to, she's picked at her food or said that it has "no taste." So we end up at Good Fortune a lot, which suits Zara and me fine, even if Mama complains about all the carbs, fat, sodium, and sugar. Tonight we're celebrating Nana Abu's seventy-third birthday.

Earlier I ran straight to Mama after I got home from school, and she was sitting in front of her computer concentrating on something.

"Did it come?" I asked.

"What, dear?"

"The e-mail! From Coach Wheeler! Did I make the team?"

"Hmmm. Let me check. I think it's right here. Oh, wait, can you hold on? I need to do something first."

"Mama! Really?" I felt like I was going to explode.

"It'll only take a second. I just need to stand up so I can . . . GIVE YOU A BIG HUG FOR MAKING THE TEAM!"

"I made it? For real?"

"For real!"

I let out a big whoop, and Mama wrapped her arms around me and squeezed me tight. Then Zara heard us and came running in, and soon we were all jumping and hugging like they do on TV sometimes. It felt great.

And now, at the restaurant with my

family around me, Jamal Mamoo tells us more news.

"I've been talking to Nadia for the past couple weeks, and she's cool."

"Oh my God! Does that mean you're getting engaged?" Zara asks.

"Not yet, but who knows. Right now I'm just getting to know a nice girl from a good family." He winks and looks at Naano when he says that last part.

"She is nice girl," she agrees. "And she has good family."

The waiter comes out with a little scoop of coconut ice cream and a lit candle in it, and we sing "Happy Birthday" to Nana Abu. Then Jamal Mamoo sings it again in a goofy mixture of English and Urdu. Nana Abu beams at us all and lets me blow out the candle.

"Thank you," he says as everyone hands

him gift bags filled with a new robe, slippers, and a book about Islamic Art. Zara and I printed out a card for him with photographs of us together, which he seems to like the best.

"And here's one for you," Jamal Mamoo says, putting a gift bag in my lap. "I'm proud of you for making the team, Skeletor," he adds. "And I'm sure you'll make the weight with all the food you just put away. Did you really eat all those noodles? Impressive, man."

I peek inside the bag and spot the logo on the box. It's a pair of Air Jordans! They are exactly the ones I wanted, black and red and perfect. I can't wait to wear them on the court and hear them squeaking. My heart beats faster as I think about showing up for the first practice with my new team.

"Thank you, Mamoo," I say. "Really. Thanks so much."

"You earned them. Now I need to see some serious balling from you."

We break into our fortune cookies next.

"Happiness comes from listening to your father," Baba pretends to read before he's even done pulling out the little paper. We all moan.

"Very funny, Baba!" Zara says.

"'You have an unusually magnetic personality.'" Naano grins as she reads hers. "Bakwas! But maybe it's good bakwas." We all laugh and agree that her fortune is legit.

"'Your smile brings happiness to everyone you meet.'" Nana Abu smiles. "Is that so?"

"Definitely!" Zara crunches her cookie. "Mine says, 'Next full moon brings you an enchanted evening.' I wonder what that will be?"

"Nothing at all, if I have anything to do with it!" Baba gives Zara an exaggerated warning look.

"I'll trade you yours for 'It is better to be the hammer than the nail,'" Jamal Mamoo offers. "What does *that* mean?"

"No thanks," Zara says. "I'm keeping mine. Let's hear yours, Zayd."

"Mama first," I say.

"'You love Chinese food,'" Mama laughs. "Okay, I confess. It's true! Sodium, carbs, and all. I love this stuff."

"And Zayd?" Baba prompts. "What does yours say?"

I swallow hard to try to clear the little lump that has formed in my throat.

"'You must power forward to achieve your dreams,'" I read in as deep a voice as I can.

"Right on!" Jamal Mamoo yells as everyone cheers for me. I take a little bow from my seat and look around as a warm feeling spreads throughout my insides. I wouldn't trade these people for anything. Okay, maybe just Zara. But only for a starting spot on the Wizards.

ON
POINT

For Bilal
—H. K.

Big-time players lean in, and I am grateful to know a few
—S. W. C.

Sometimes when you finally get something you really want, it ends up not being what you hoped it would be. Like that remote-control car that's supposed to be able to drive over anything but gets stuck on the carpet and spins its wheels. Or the haircut that is cool looking on that kid on TV but on you looks like a giant mushroom sprouted on top of your head.

So far, though, being on my new basketball team is as amazing as I thought it would be. It's totally worth the weeks of practice I put into getting ready for tryouts. And that includes getting grounded when I skipped violin practice to play basketball instead. I'm finally on the best team in the fourth-grade league with my best friend, Adam. And each time I lace up my sneakers and step onto the gym floor during practice, I feel like a million bucks.

It's halftime during our first game of the season. My parents and older sister, Zara, are in the stands. I heard them cheering loudly for me when Coach Wheeler put me in during the last five minutes of the first half. I missed a wide-open shot but had a good pass and a nice rebound. And now I get to start the second half!

My heart is thumping wildly in my chest. This is exactly the moment I've been waiting for.

We're huddled around Coach and his clipboard, where he scribbles down plays and taps his pen to make his point. We're down by four. Not too bad. Although by the way Coach is speaking, you'd think we were losing by a lot.

"All right, guys." Coach Wheeler taps on the clipboard. "I know we have new players. We're still learning to work together as a team. That's no excuse for rushing your passes and turning the ball over. Remember to keep the ball up when you rebound."

I look around at my new teammates' faces. Adam looks determined. Blake is super sweaty. Ravindu looks like he hasn't slept enough. And Sam? He's mouthing something to his mom in the bleachers instead of paying attention.

"Who's going to take us home?" Coach asks.

MD HOOPS!!!

"Let's do this," Adam says gruffly. He's the team captain, and he puts his hand out first. I stick mine on top of his, and soon there's a pile of hands.

"One, two, three, MD HOOPS!" we shout in unison. I feel reenergized as I step back onto the court. I'm going to put up some serious points in the second half. I can feel it.

Blake inbounds the ball, and Adam starts to take it up the court. I always admire his handles. He can dribble behind his back, and he has a sweet crossover. He's stuck right now, though, because the other team is pressing him hard. Two guys are all over him.

"Over here," I yell, holding out my hands. Adam glances at me for a second but then flings the ball over to Blake. A kid from the other team strips it from Blake before he has possession. The kid takes it down the court on a fast break and makes an easy layup. Now we're down by six.

We get the ball back, and this time Adam passes it to me. I immediately have two guys smothering me. All I can see is a bunch of arms waving in my face like a giant octopus. They've got me in a trap, and I try to pass the ball back to Adam. But I turn the ball over. The other team runs down the court and puts up two more points. Now we're down eight.

My dad loves this old movie where this guy wakes up each morning and the same thing happens to him over and over again. It sounds super boring to me, but now I know what he means when he says, "This reminds me of *Groundhog Day.*" Because the same exact pattern keeps repeating. We get the ball. They press us. We turn the ball over. They score. Repeat.

We're down by twelve with only three minutes left.

"Time out!" Coach yells. He looks as sweaty as we are and has been pacing the sidelines and yelling louder as each minute ticks by.

"Let's see if you guys have better luck," he mutters as he puts in the entire bench for the rest of the game. Adam and I sit next to Blake, Sam, and Ravindu and watch as our teammates try to shake things up. It doesn't work. We end up losing 32–17.

This isn't how I imagined playing on the gold team would feel. They were undefeated last season and got second place in the playoffs. I thought I'd be playing on *that* team. Today feels like I got another mushroom haircut.

2

"Spicy sauce, please," I say to the guy behind the counter making my pizza. We're at Pie Echo, my new favorite place to eat out. You pick the toppings you want on your pizza, and they put it together and cook it in a super-fast oven that makes the crust bubble and cheese melt in less than five minutes.

This restaurant is perfect for my family since we can never agree on what we want for delivery. Here, Mama can get an entire salad on her pizza, Zara can go crazy with pineapple, and Baba and I can load up on meatballs, jalapeños, and four kinds of cheese. The whole family leaves happy.

"No veggies for you, either, Adam?" Mama looks at Adam's pizza and raises an eyebrow. He came with us for a late lunch after our game. That's been one of the best parts of being on the gold team together. Now we get to hang out even more than before, including carpooling to practice and games. Having Adam at lunch helps to make up for today's loss.

"Tomato sauce is made of veggies," Adam replies with a smile. He's assembled a totally plain cheese pizza. Even I have to admit it looks kind of boring when there are twenty-five different toppings to pick from.

"Whatever you're eating is working," Baba agrees. "You're going to be as tall as me pretty soon!"

Adam's always been taller than me, but suddenly he towers over me by at least a foot. I can't wait until I finally hit that "growth spurt" I always hear about. I've managed to put on a few pounds and finally passed the sixty-pound mark. Even still, the line on the wall in my home where we keep track of my height is hardly budging.

The door opens, and my grandparents come shuffling into the restaurant and look around for us.

"Salaams! You made it!" Zara jumps up to give our grandfather, Nana Abu, her seat and pulls up a chair for Naano. Mama said it would be too hard for them to come to both my game and lunch. So they picked lunch. I don't mind. They don't follow basketball or care much about it, and the bleachers are uncomfortable. Although, I suddenly realize that my uncle, Jamal Mamoo, said he was going to try to be at my game, and he didn't show up.

"Wait, don't sit down. Our pizzas are coming out in a minute. Come up to the counter and let's make yours," Mama says.

Nana Abu sits down anyway and smiles at us.

"We make pizza? They don't make pizza?" Naano asks. She looks appalled.

"No, Naano," I explain. "They make it for you, after you tell them what you want."

"I want onion and mushroom." Naano sits down too.

"What about you, Abu?" Mama asks.

"Anything is fine," he says. Clearly, they aren't interested in walking any farther.

"Okay, come help me, Zayd." While my mom and I are choosing the pizza toppings for my grandparents, Jamal Mamoo walks into the restaurant.

"Hey, Skeletor." He gives me a bro hug and uses his favorite nickname for me. "How was the game?"

"Don't ask."

"Good thing I slept through it, then," he says, laughing. "Mmm. Pizza works for breakfast."

"It's three in the afternoon, Jamal," Mama scolds. "You know this schedule of yours isn't going to work when you're married."

"Married!" I scoff. "Good thing that's not happening anytime soon."

Mama and Jamal Mamoo exchange a look.

"Wait. What's going on?" I ask.

"Let's sit down," mamoo says. "I have some news."

Back at the table I feel my pizza gurgling in my stomach as Jamal Mamoo explains that he is getting engaged to Nadia, the girl my family literally JUST went to meet together.

"Mamoo, it's only been, what, a month or two? How can you know you want to marry her already?" I look around at my family. They have to agree that this is madness. Naano and Nana Abu aren't fazed the slightest bit. Zara is beaming at mamoo. Baba seems amused.

I turn to Adam, and he shrugs.

"Dude, don't ask me," he says, his mouth full of pizza.

"Mamoo, really," I say. "Don't you think this is kind of . . . fast?"

"I know it sounds rushed," Jamal Mamoo says.

"What's rushed about it?" Naano says. "I talked to your father two times before we got married."

Adam's jaw drops. "Really?" he whispers to me.

"We've been talking a lot, and we're on the same page about what we want out of life. We laugh a lot, and I know she's the one," Jamal Mamoo continues.

"OH MY GOD!" Zara looks ready to explode. "This is so exciting!"

"I know!" Mama grins. "We're going to have a wedding! We'll get outfits made for the whole family. Maybe the guys can wear suits. Zayd, I wonder where I can get you a suit that isn't too expensive."

"I have a suit I wore last year to my brother's bar mitzvah," Adam offers. "It'll probably fit you."

"Oh, that's nice of you, Adam!" Mama gushes. The rest of lunch all the family wants to

150

talk about is the engagement. Luckily, I have Adam with me. He and I come up with crazy drink combinations at the soda machine since no one is paying attention to us. The best are cherry peach Sprite and vanilla root beer.

It's too bad life doesn't work the same way as the soda fountain or the pizza at Pie Echo. You don't always get to pick what you want. Suddenly mine includes a losing start to the season, a way-too-fast wedding, and a hand-me-down suit.

3

Recess is our reward for having to be at school the whole day. At least it is on the days when it isn't too rainy or too cold to go outside to play. Today is one of those days. I see the sun shining through the window and watch the clock slowly tick down during social studies. I can't wait to rush outside and grab a basketball and a court before they're snatched up.

"What are you doing?" I ask Blake when the bell finally rings and we can line up. He hasn't packed up his stuff.

"I'm not ready for the geography test," Blake says. "I did bad on the review sheet. I need to get help."

"Seriously?" Adam asks. "It's only about directions."

"I got half wrong. I don't get it."

"We can help you. It's easy," I offer. I point in front of us. "If that's north, which way is east?"

"That way," Blake points.

"Right. You got it. Let's go play." I start to leave.

"Wait. Give me another." Blake stops me.

"Okay, if that's north, and you're walking

in the opposite direction, which way are you going?" I say.

"North."

"Dude. I said north is the other way." I give him a friendly punch.

"But I'm facing this way." Blake looks confused.

Adam shakes his head. "There's only one north."

"I know," Blake says. "There's only one north. Which is whichever way I'm facing."

"You think north is whatever way you're facing?" I can't believe what I'm hearing. "You're kidding, right?"

"No. Wait. What do you mean?" Blake turns red.

"Wow," Adam adds. "You can't be serious. Are you serious?"

"You guys are confusing me," Blake whines.

"Go get help, Blake," Adam looks at the clock. "And then hurry up and come outside. We'll be on the court waiting for you. Just head *north*, and you'll find it."

Blake makes a face, and Adam and I rush outside to the basketball court. A bunch of guys are already there, shooting around.

"Where's Blake?" Keanu asks.

"He's . . . uh . . . lost right now." Adam smiles at me. "Let's start without him."

"But we need another," Keanu says.

"Let's play two-on-three until Blake gets here. Me and Zayd versus you three."

"Are you sure?" Chris says.

"Yeah." Adam looks at me. "Right?"

"Sure," I agree, although I don't think it's an even matchup. Keanu and Chris are in the developmental league I used to be a part of. They didn't make the gold team with me, but they're still good. And they have Sam, who's on our team *and* better than me.

But as we start to play, Adam and I are amazing. He starts off by making a smooth bounce pass, setting me up for an easy layup.

"Nice pass," I say as Adam gives me a high five.

The next play I manage to steal the ball from Keanu, get by Chris, and pass it to Adam. He makes a jump shot near the free throw line. It would be a swish if there were any nets on the hoops.

"Oh yeah!" Adam shouts.

It's as if Adam can read my mind and knows when I'm going to make a move to get open. On the court, I imagine we're my favorite duo, John Wall and Bradley Beal on the Wizards. When they're in sync, they're unstoppable.

"Come on, guys," Chris yells at his teammates. "These two can't beat us."

But we totally do. By a lot. Even without Blake. And when he finally comes out and sheepishly says he understands which way is north now, we're already up by eight. I'm sure that if we play this way during our next game, we'll definitely be headed in the right direction.

4

Everyone is talking at the same time, and no one is listening to each other. They especially aren't listening to Jamal Mamoo, even though we're supposed to be talking about *his* wedding.

"We need to find a caterer or hall with halal food," Mama says.

"Nadia and I were thinking of gourmet southern comfort food," Jamal Mamoo suggests. "Like some shrimp and grits and cornbread."

"Southern food, shmuthern food!" Naano snorts. "If you don't serve proper Pakistani dinner no one will enjoy."

"I want to try shmuthern food," I say.

Zara and I look at each other and smile.

"Butthameez!" Naano scolds me with an Urdu word that means "naughty boy" or something like that.

"Yeah, you're a BUTT-thameez," Zara says, and we both laugh "like hyenas" according to Naano.

"Can we talk about this wedding guest list?" Jamal Mamoo pleads. He doesn't join in the joking like usual. "I don't even know half these people. Nadia and I want to keep it small. Only close friends and family."

"It will be small," Naano says. "Don't take tension. No more than two hundred people."

"Two hundred!" Beads of sweat form on Jamal Mamoo's forehead, and he looks totally stressed out now. "We wanted around seventy-five."

"But your father and I have fifty, and that's only our friends."

"Help me. Please." Jamal Mamoo gives Mama a desperate look. "Nadia's family has to invite their people too. And what about my friends?"

"Let's take a break and have some chai." Mama nods at mamoo and pats him on the shoulder as she gets up to go to the kitchen.

"Can we go outside now?" I ask. Mamoo promised me we'd play some one-on-one, and I've been waiting forever.

"Not yet, Skeletor. We still have a lot of details to work out."

"But this is boring." I can't help complaining. Ever since mamoo mentioned getting engaged, it's the only thing anyone is talking about. And no one has even picked a wedding date yet.

"I know." Jamal Mamoo grimaces. "No one's listening to anything I'm saying anyway. But we need to figure this stuff out. We'll play when we're done."

"Zayd! Can you give me a hand?" Mama calls me from the kitchen before I have a chance to go outside by myself.

I walk into the kitchen, and Mama already has a pot of water and tea leaves simmering on the stove. She pours milk into the pot and stands over it until it starts to boil. I've seen her turn around and not catch the chai from bubbling up and overflowing onto the stove a million times. There's got to be a better way where that doesn't happen. But this is how Naano likes her chai best, and the only way our family makes it.

"Can you get out the sugar and some biscuits?" Mama asks.

I arrange a plate of butter biscuits on a worn metal tray and eat a couple in the process.

"How come mamoo can't make the wedding any way he wants?" I ask when I'm done chewing.

"What do you mean?" Mama asks me, without taking her eyes off the tea.

"I mean he's a grown-up. I get to choose who I want to invite to my birthday parties and what kind of pizza and cake I want. Why doesn't he get to pick what he wants for his own wedding?"

Mama laughs.

"I'm serious," I say. "I don't get it."

"Well . . ." Mama grows thoughtful. "I guess this is more of a team party. Naano and Nana Abu are excited that their only son is getting married, and they want to share their joy with their friends."

"Well the marriage team isn't fun. Jamal Mamoo should quit."

"Shh! Don't give him any ideas. I have my own list of people to invite too. Plus we haven't even talked about decorations or outfits yet."

I look over at Jamal Mamoo, arguing about how he doesn't think he can rent a horse to ride to the wedding like they do in Pakistan. I bet he had no idea this marriage stuff would be this difficult. I hope he figures it out soon. And that he hurries up so we can go outside to play before it gets too dark.

5

"We're going to focus on breaking the press today," Coach Wheeler announces at the start of practice. "That game was rough. We have to work harder to make sure it doesn't happen again."

Everyone sneaks glances at Adam as Coach

speaks. Adam stares straight ahead with a challenging look on his face. It's not exactly fair. The way we lost wasn't only his fault. But since he's our starting point guard, and the one holding the ball most of the time when it got stripped or stolen, he ended up looking the worst.

"Split into two groups," Coach directs us. "Half of you press, and the other half run the press break."

I move with Adam to the press-break group. We have to get the ball to Adam for him to make a move and pass it to someone in the middle of the court. And the other half of the team tries to stop us by being extremely aggressive and not letting us move the ball.

"Go!" Coach shouts.

Cody starts and inbounds the ball. Immediately Blake and Sam start to smother Adam.

He dribbles and tries to cut to his right, but Blake steals the ball from him and takes it down for a fast-break layup. I have a flashback to our *Groundhog Day* game over the weekend. That's exactly what happened to us over and over again.

Coach blows his whistle.

"Adam, try dribbling lower. Make it harder for the other team to steal the ball. Maybe you draw a foul instead of giving up the ball."

"Got it." Adam nods his head.

We start again. This time I inbound the ball past Sam, who is in my face. I barely get it to Adam within the five-second limit.

Adam dribbles between his legs and starts to cut to his left. I run up and get open, Adam makes a quick pass to me, and instantly two guys are covering me tight. I have nowhere to go and try to pass the ball back to Adam. Blake intercepts my pass and is gone again.

"Zayd!" Adam points to where Cody was standing. "You should have passed to Cody."

I didn't see Cody or think he was open. Maybe he was.

"Sorry," I say.

"Guys, listen up. You need to spread out and keep moving. If you end up getting double-teamed, make sure you wait for your teammate to cut and get open. Don't throw a rushed pass." Coach Wheeler sounds as frustrated as I feel.

We run the drill a few more times, and each time something goes wrong. And then we switch up the groups, this time with Sam playing point and us pressing. That goes about the same.

Coach blows his whistle again.

"Let's take a break and work on dribbling and making offensive cuts. Remember, keep the ball low to the floor."

Adam mutters under his breath. "I do keep the ball low."

"Hey," I say to him. "He's saying it to the whole team."

"I know." Adam shakes his head. "But no one gets open. I have nobody to pass to when I'm double-teamed. Our team was much better last season."

Ouch. I don't think he means to say that the team was better before I was on it. Or that it's worse BECAUSE

I'm on it. But his words still sting.

I don't say anything else and work on my moves the way Coach instructs us. We have to figure out how to break the press. And get open quicker. And dribble low. And rebound high. My head is spinning with all the instructions. I'm also going to pray that the next team we play isn't as good as we are. I want the gold team to start winning again. And I want Adam to think this team—with me on it—is even better than the old one.

6

Wednesdays are the best day of the week. Not only do we have gym class in the afternoon, but it's also chorus day. I'm not in the chorus, but since most of my math class is, it means the handful of us that are left get free time. Sometimes we do homework. Or, when Mr.

Thomas is in a good mood, he lets us go to math websites on classroom tablets or do other fun stuff.

"Can we play SMATH?" Adam asks Mr. Thomas. He holds up a box of a math board game.

"Did you finish your worksheet?" Mr. Thomas asks from his desk, where he's grading tests.

"Yup."

"Okay. Keep it down, though. Some of the others are still working."

Adam motions to Blake, Keanu, and me to follow him into the cubby area.

"That game is boring," Keanu complains.

"I know. We're not going to play it," Adam says in a low voice. He pulls a deck of cards out of his backpack. "Grab those Connect Four pieces."

We set the board game up as if we are going to play it. But then we huddle behind it in the cubby area and play poker. Adam divides up the Connect Four pieces as poker chips.

"The black pieces are worth ten dollars, and the red are worth twenty," he explains.

Adam taught me how to play poker during indoor recess earlier in the year. I'm still not that good at it. He's amazing and always seems to win. Win or lose, I'm sure poker is way more fun than SMATH.

"I see your twenty, and I raise you another twenty," Keanu says.

"I'm out," I say as I put down my cards. "I've got nothing."

"Call." Adam puts in his red chip.

"BOYS!" We hear a voice behind us and freeze. It's Mr. Thomas.

"I said you could play the math game! What are you doing?"

"Poker's a math game too," Adam says. "Right? We have to count and stuff."

Mr. Thomas turns red.

"I gave you permission to play SMATH," he says. "But you're being sneaky and playing cards instead?"

"Sorry," we mumble.

"I'm going to have to write you up for being off task and dishonest."

I look at Adam in a panic. I've never gotten a pink slip before. But Adam brushes it off.

Mr. Thomas hands me the slip with a disappointed frown as I leave class for lunch.

"Make sure you show this to a parent and get a signature. And next time I expect you to do what you say you will."

"I will," I say, and then I shove the slip into my binder.

"My parents are going to freak out," I say as I catch up to Adam.

"Just sign it yourself," he says. "That's what I'm going to do."

"No way. I promised my parents to be honest. I'm not getting grounded again." I suddenly realize that when I got into trouble for skipping violin practice to play basketball it was also Adam's idea.

"We were playing cards. You weren't cheating on a test or anything."

I stare at my friend. Why is he acting like he's some tough guy?

"Is everything okay with you?" I ask.

"Yeah. Why?"

"Nothing."

I figure he'll snap out of it. But when we

go out to recess, instead of running to claim a basketball court, he turns to me.

"I'm going to play football with Antonio and Charlie," he says.

"Why?" I can't believe what I'm hearing. We play basketball whenever we go outside.

"I played football yesterday when I was waiting to get picked up after Spanish class, and it was fun."

"Okay." I don't know what else to say, even though it's *not* okay. Not one bit. I pause to see if Adam will ask me if I want to play football with him, but he doesn't. It's not like I want to play with them anyway. Antonio is the biggest kid in the fourth grade, and he plays real football with pads and helmets in some league. I heard he gave a kid a concussion from hitting him too hard. Even though these guys play two-hand touch at recess, they still come

in with grass stains and muddy shoes and scrapes. Besides, I'd rather play basketball any chance I can get.

I watch Adam walk toward the ball rack, pick up a football, and jog off to the field. Between the pink slip and the weird attitude he's having, this Wednesday is the worst.

7

I walk into the house and drop my backpack by the door. Mama and Naano are in the kitchen drinking chai.

"What's the matter?" Mama asks when she sees my face. "You feeling okay?"

I shake my head no.

"What's wrong?" Mama comes close to me and puts her hand on my forehead as if she is checking for a fever.

"I got a . . ."

"What?" Mama looks anxious. "You don't feel warm."

"Pink slip. Even though I didn't do anything bad! Promise. We were playing cards and Mr. Thomas got mad." I say it as quickly as I can.

"What? Show it to me."

"You got a PINK SLIP? Whoa. I *never* got one of those when I was in elementary school."

Zara is sitting at the table eating celery smeared with peanut butter, and she jumps up and comes over to us.

I fumble through my backpack and slowly pull out the pink slip. Zara grabs it out of my hand and starts to read it aloud.

"'Zayd failed to follow directions and stay on task. Please discuss the importance of being honest with him.'"

"Give that to me." Mama holds out her hand. Then she looks at me sternly. "Explain."

"When the people who are in chorus leave, sometimes Mr. Thomas lets the rest of us play games. He said we could play this math game, but we played poker instead."

"You gamble at school?" Naano interrupts. "How much money you make?"

"No, Naano. Not for money. For fun. With Connect Four chips."

"Pshhh." Naano looks disappointed.

"Ammi, let me talk to Zayd, please," Mama pleads. "Remember gambling is haram?"

"That's only if you lose,"

Naano retorts, which makes Mama wince.

"Go on, Zayd," Mama says. "So you weren't playing for money?"

"No! Mr. Thomas got mad at us for not playing the math game."

"What math game?" I can tell Mama doesn't quite believe me.

"It's called SMATH. You make equations. Keanu says it's boring."

"So you played poker instead?"

"Yeah. We were still doing math, kind of. When we were betting. You have to count and stuff."

"You count cards and make lots of money," Naano says with a wink. "I show you how to play twenty-one."

"Ammi, please." Mama frowns, but her eyes are smiling. "And then?"

"Then he caught us and said we were

getting pink slips. He acted like his feelings were hurt."

Mama reads the pink slip and lets out a sigh. I hold my breath, waiting for a lecture on honesty and respect, and wonder what my punishment will be. Then, miraculously, she simply pulls a pen out of the drawer and signs the slip.

"Here you go." She hands it back to me. "Next time do what you said you were going to do. Be good. And don't disappoint your teacher."

"That's it?" I ask.

"Yeah? That's *it*?" Zara asks. She waves her celery in the air. "Doesn't he get in trouble? He got a pink slip!"

"Excuse me, Zara. This doesn't concern you," Mama says. "Zayd, did you learn your lesson?"

"Yeah."

"Okay then. Don't do it again. And I don't want to see any more pink slips."

"Okay."

PHEW! I was expecting a bigger a reaction, but I'll take this. I guess Mama doesn't think sneaking a different game during math is as big a deal as sneaking into the gym to play basketball instead of going to violin lessons for two weeks. And I'm not going to remind her about that.

Naano winks at me again.

"Next time you make money at school, I get half," she says.

Mama sighs louder. I give Naano a high five and then rummage through the pantry for something to eat other than celery.

8

"Did you see the first half of the game last night?" I ask Adam as we file out to recess the next day. "That was crazy when John Wall jumped over those people in the stands. I can't believe he didn't crush anyone."

"Or that he didn't get hurt. My dad says

he's too reckless," Adam says.

"No he isn't. He's amazing," I argue. Wall turned the game around when the Wizards were down by ten, and they came back to win. He's the best point guard I've ever seen. The fans in the stands were shouting "MVP" loud enough for us to hear them on TV.

"Catch you after recess," Adam says, veering away from me.

"What are you doing? You're playing basketball today, right?" I ask, following him.

"Nah. I'm going to play football again." Adam nods over to where Antonio and Charlie are standing by the wall, waiting for him with a football. I realize that means they must have already talked about it.

"But we need you to make the teams even," I protest.

"Ask Ravindu. He'll probably play." Adam points.

I look over to where Ravindu is kicking a soccer ball against the brick wall with another boy. He's good at every sport and on our basketball team. I'm cool playing with him, although it's not the same as playing with Adam.

"Come on." I try to convince him. "We were awesome last time we played at recess. Remember?"

"Yeah." Adam glances at Antonio, who is waving him over. "But . . . those guys are waiting for me."

"We're waiting for you too." What's going on with Adam? Something doesn't feel right.

"I don't get to play football that much. It's fun. Antonio says I'd make an awesome receiver."

"Antonio's not the boss of you." I blurt that out when I can't think of anything else to say.

"Neither are you," Adam snaps back. "Why are you freaking out about this?"

My face gets hot, and I clench my fists tight.

"We ALWAYS play basketball." I kind of yell it. I can't even believe I have to say any of this. We've been playing basketball during recess for two years. It's what we always do.

"Yeah. That's why I'm playing football. Chill, Zayd."

Our team's second game of the season was Sunday afternoon. It was pretty much a repeat of the week before. Anything that could go wrong did. We kept turning the ball over, missing our shots, giving up the fast break, and playing horribly. And we lost 29–15. When we huddled up after the game, Adam wouldn't look at anyone. He looked upset enough to cry. Since I felt the same way, I didn't think anything of it.

But now I ask him, "How are we supposed to figure out how to win again if we don't play?"

"That's what practice is for. I need a break." Adam starts to walk away.

"JOHN WALL WOULDN'T DITCH HIS TEAM!" I shout as I stand there and glare at him.

"WHATEVER!" he barks back without even turning around to look at me.

Maybe Adam doesn't think he's being the worst friend *ever*. But that doesn't change the fact that he is.

"Ravindu! Can you play ball with us?" I pant, out of breath from yelling and running over to him.

"Yeah." Ravindu leaves the soccer ball mid-roll and runs to the court with me.

"Where's Adam?" Blake asks.

"Playing football again," I mutter.

Blake shrugs. "Let's go," he says.

We split up to play three-on-three. It's Ravindu, Chris, and me versus Keanu, Blake, and Sam. Maybe it's because I'm angry with Adam, but something seems to take over me. I'm playing more aggressively than I ever have, boxing out, grabbing every rebound, making crazy passes, and taking shots that I would normally never try. I feel incredible.

But then I look over at the football field and watch Adam catch a long pass.

9

I get home from school, have a quick snack, and change into my training jersey for practice. Then I lace up the Jordans that Jamal Mamoo got me as a prize for hitting sixty pounds and making the gold team. I never wear them to school since I don't want them to get scuffed or dirty during recess or gym class. I grab a water bottle and my jacket and tell my mom I'm ready to go.

When we get into the car, Mama starts to drive in the direction of practice.

"You forgot to turn. We have to pick up Adam," I say.

"Oh, he didn't tell you?" Mama asks. "His mom texted me to say he's not coming to practice today."

"No." I think back to today. After recess we avoided each other for the rest of the afternoon. It was pretty easy to do since we had to work on our country study and broke into small groups. Adam and I are in different groups. Then, after the bell rang, he rushed out to catch his bus. We didn't talk again.

But now not only did he not play with us at recess, he's not coming to practice, either?

Is it because of our argument? Is he still mad at me? Now I wonder if I shouldn't have said anything to him about playing football and let it go instead. I start to worry. Our team needs Adam like the Wizards need John Wall! And I still need my friend.

When I get to practice, Coach Wheeler sits us on the court and gives us another talk.

"Things didn't go our way last game." He starts by stating the obvious. "But we have to learn from our mistakes and try new things. Today we're going to switch up positions and see if that works better for us."

I've been playing small forward and can't imagine Coach will put me in another position. I'm not tall enough to be center or power forward. That's clearly Matthew or Blake. Adam is our point guard, and Sam subs in for him. I guess maybe I could move

to shooting guard? Coach looks at me first.

"Zayd, I want you on point."

"Me?" I can't help but blurt that out. Is he serious? I look around to see if the rest of the team is as surprised as me. No one seems to think it's a big deal.

"Yeah. Blake, you play center. Ravindu, you're small forward. Sam, you're shooting guard. And Matthew's power forward. You with me?"

"Yes, Coach," we reply in unison. I start to sweat buckets. Me on point? I don't have the handles that Adam does. And to be completely honest, I don't think I'm at Sam's level either. I know I can pass and shoot. I'm trying to be more consistent at getting boards. And I hustle on defense. But putting me in charge of moving the ball up the court? That is not going to help our team start winning. Especially if we get pressed! I don't have the moves to get around two people.

"Let's run four-out," Coach says. I pause for a second, wondering if I should say something to him when no one else is listening? Coach Wheeler won't like being questioned. I imagine the look of disgust on his face if I were to tell him I don't think I'm ready. So I don't.

Coach blows the whistle, and we begin a drill where I start with the ball and then pass it to Ravindu on the wing. Then I run toward Sam and set a screen for him. Ravindu makes a move and passes the ball to Sam. We keep passing the ball around until Matthew makes a shot and it goes in.

"Nice job," Coach says with a nod toward me. "Do it again."

We do the drill over and over. The whole time, I'm comparing myself to Adam. I know he dribbles better than me with his left hand. And he's a lot smoother with his moves. I've always looked up to him for the way he commands the court.

But now Adam isn't here, and I'm left trying to fill his shoes. It doesn't feel right. Besides, what'll happen when he comes back to practice? I hope he won't think it was MY idea and that I tried to steal his spot. I start to sweat again as I picture that scene playing out.

"Let's stick with this for the next week, guys," Coach Wheeler says. "We have a bye week. No game this weekend. So we have more time to prepare. Who wants to take us out?"

I hesitate, and Blake puts his hand out first. The rest of us pile our hands in the middle and shout, "One, two, three, MD Hoops!" I might mumble it. If Adam hasn't been able to lead us to victory, how in the world can I be expected to? I hope he comes back. And quick.

10

My dad has a rule: absolutely no whining or complaining allowed when we go on road trips. Today it's Naano who keeps asking how much longer the ride will be. The rest of the time, she's telling him how to drive. Every couple of minutes she bursts out with "Slow down!" "Watch out!" or "You're too close!" If someone else on the road does something she doesn't like, she rattles off a bunch of curse words in Urdu that I'm pretty sure are way worse than BUTT-thameez.

I can tell by the wrinkles on Baba's forehead and the way he's squishing his lips together that she's frustrating him. And I'm pretty sure that he wants to get to New Jersey as quickly as possible.

My entire family, Jamal Mamoo, Naano, and Nana Abu are crammed into our minivan on an epic adventure to buy stuff for Jamal Mamoo's engagement. It was all Naano's big idea. She heard that the best shop for Pakistani sweets is in this magical place called Edison in New Jersey that I've never been to before.

"We will get mithai and give it to our friends to announce the engagement," she said, while Jamal Mamoo complained.

"Can't we give chocolates instead? No one actually *eats* mithai," he said.

I agreed. I've tried all different types of mithai—pretty much every desi celebration serves it. The colorful super-sweet sweets come in different shapes and flavors. Some are syrupy donuts that are pretty decent. Others are crumbly blocks of candied cheese called burfy. I'm not even making that up. And they taste as gross as that sounds. But Naano made up her mind. She's not going to give up tradition. And she doesn't want any old regular mithai. Nothing but the best will do for her friends, even if that means driving from Maryland to New Jersey for it.

Mama and Zara got super excited about the Indian and Pakistani boutiques and jewelry shops in Edison. Nana Abu and Baba had heard of some famous kabob restaurant called Bundoo Khan they wanted to try. I was probably the least excited about the whole trip, but Mama tried to convince me it would be fun.

"Pretend we're going to Pakistan, without getting on a plane. The shops and restaurants are similar to the ones in Lahore," she said. "We'll get roasted corn and the best kulfi ever."

I've never been to Pakistan and don't know what to expect. Roasted corn and creamy kulfi popsicles don't sound bad, though. I was sold.

Now, after three cramped hours in the car, between Naano's backseat driving, Nana Abu's snoring, and the fact that I left my headphones at home, I'm ready to *get there already*. Jamal Mamoo has hardly talked to me, since he's been texting Nadia Auntie the whole ride.

When we finally pull off the highway, a taxicab cuts us off, and Baba swerves the tiniest bit to avoid it. *SMACK!* Naano grabs the seat in front of her and slams on an imaginary brake with her leg. And then somehow she manages to pray and curse in the same sentence. Zara giggles, and Baba shakes his head.

"We're here," he says with a dramatic hand wave.

We've pulled up in front of Bundoo Khan, which doesn't seem special from the outside. Baba parks on the street, and we pile out of the minivan, tired, hungry, and wrinkled. We file in together, and the smell of masala, fried onions, and barbequed meat hits my nostrils. A man nods us over to a table covered in a clear plastic tablecloth with red placemats underneath.

As we settle in, Nana Abu transforms into someone I've never seen before. My quiet, soft-spoken grandfather is a boss at Bundoo Khan. The waiters rush to him when he looks in their direction, bow their heads when he speaks, and keep asking if there is anything else he wants. He seems to have grown a few inches taller as he orders plates of kabob and rice and asks them to make something that isn't even on the menu.

"What's up with Nana Abu?" I whisper to Zara.

"I don't know," she says. "Maybe it's because it's like we're in Pakistan?"

Then the food starts to come out in metal dishes with handles on them sitting in woven baskets. The reddish tandoori chicken is the best I've ever had in my life—even better than my and Jamal Mamoo's favorite chicken place, Crisp & Juicy. The meat is barbequed perfectly and falls off the bone. It doesn't even need any sauce.

Nana Abu orders naan that has garlic baked

into it and channa masala and curried lamb chops. The dishes keep coming, and we stuff ourselves until my jeans start to feel too tight. It's a spread like Thanksgiving dinner, only a lot spicier. Plus instead of football, there is a cricket match playing on the enormous TV on the wall. When we insist we can't eat any more, the waiters clear the table and bring us glass dishes with rice pudding in them for free.

"This is incredible!" Somehow Zara eats her entire bowl and then finishes Mama's, too. The rest of us can only manage a bite and then look at one another with satisfied-but-slightly-pained expressions. It sounds crazy, but this meal was worth the drive. All three hours of it.

"Let's go," Mama says as she pays the bill. "We have work to do. And we have to make room for kulfi in a few hours."

11

Mama wasn't kidding that Edison could be "Little Pakistan." As we walk down the street, the stores have names like Shalimar Sweets, Saree Bazaar, Maharani Fashions, and Raj Jewels. The mannequins in the windows are wearing fancy shalwar kameezes. Posters of

Bollywood movies and Indian variety shows are plastered everywhere. And there are so many people who look like they could be straight out of Naano's favorite Pakistani dramas walking around.

While Naano, Nana Abu, and Baba head to the sweet store to get mithai, I go with Mama, Zara, and Jamal Mamoo to explore a few boutiques to look for outfits for the wedding.

"Oh, congratulations!" coos a middle-aged woman wearing glasses decorated with sparkling stones when Mama tells her that Jamal Mamoo is getting married.

"Big party?" she asks. Jamal Mamoo shakes his head no, and Mama nods her head yes at the same time.

"Let's see what we have for the handsome groom-to-be," the lady gushes. I can't tell for sure since his skin is dark, but I think Jamal Mamoo might be blushing.

"Check out these shoes, Mamoo," I laugh, holding up a pair of fancy silver slippers that curl up in the front. They resemble what a prince might wear, or the genie from *Aladdin*.

"'A whole new world . . .'" I sing a line from the Disney movie in a fake deep voice, expecting mamoo to bust out with his usual loud wacky laugh. Instead, he barely looks in my direction and continues to listen to the lady make suggestions on the latest in Indian fashion.

"'A new fantastic point of view,'" Zara sings, picking up where I left off. She takes the shoes from me and puts them on. And then we search for other stuff.

I find a super-chunky necklace and a fancy twisted turban and put them on, and Zara finds a bejeweled scarf. We take selfies and videos with Zara's phone and then put all sorts of silly filters on them. We're laughing really hard, and I haven't had this much fun with Zara in a long time. But then Mama calls

her to try on an outfit, and I'm left standing alone in my turban. Mama looks over at me, and her eyes grow big.

"Put that back," she mouths to me.

Mamoo comes out of the dressing room wearing a kurta that is a shimmery dark pink with embroidery on it. There's a cream color scarf draped around his shoulders. He looks at the ladies with a doubtful expression, and they start to gush over him.

"That's perfect," the lady says.

"You think?" mamoo says. "I don't know. It's a bit much."

"Don't you think that's too shiny?" I ask. "Are you seriously letting them dress you up? I thought you were going to wear a suit with me."

Mamoo doesn't even answer me. Instead, he asks Zara to take a picture of him in his getup, and he sends it to Nadia Auntie. Then he gets on the phone with her and starts having a long conversation about what color she will be wearing and what will look good together. Mama is talking to the sparkly eyeglasses lady about the wedding decorations and what will look best, like nothing mamoo says counts at all.

"Can we go now?" I ask my mom.

"In a bit," she says. "Do these look fake?" She holds up a pair of earrings that are in the shape of tiny chandeliers.

"I don't know," I say. And then I pull out my secret weapon. "I need the bathroom."

"Really? You have to go *now*?"

"Yup."

"Can you hold it?"

"No. I have to go bad," I say, putting on a desperate look.

Mama asks the lady if there's a bathroom we can use, and she points to the café across the street. Freedom! We tell Zara and mamoo to meet us there and head over to Agha Juice Bar. I quickly take care of business while Mama orders me a kulfi and herself a falooda, which is a milkshake with red syrup and spaghetti-like noodles in it.

As we walk outside, and I enjoy my sweet milky popsicle, we find the rest of the family standing in front of a man with a cart, putting something together that I've never seen before.

"What is that?"

"It's called paan," Baba says. "It's for grown-ups."

I don't understand how it's for anybody. Paan is a big leaf—as in the thing that comes off a tree. The guy fills the inside of it with a bunch of seeds and syrups and dried coconut that Naano chooses and rolls it up into a tiny triangle burrito. Naano pays him and pops the whole thing into her mouth, which turns a dark orange color from the syrup.

Zara and I look at each other in disbelief as Naano smacks her lips with pleasure. Then she and I go back into the café to get her a kulfi. We help load the mithai and the other packages into the car and start the long drive back. Everyone looks full and satisfied, except for Jamal Mamoo, who falls asleep with his forehead still crinkled up with worry.

12

I've only missed the bus a couple of times before. I ran out of the house and saw the yellow end of the bus turning onto the next street. I tried chasing it the first time, but now I know that I can't catch up. Our driver takes off like she's in a high-speed chase or trying to win the Daytona 500.

Today was another time I missed the bus. I didn't even get outside. Instead, I hit the wrong button on my alarm clock and was still dreaming long after the bus left. Then I heard Baba exclaiming, "Zayd! Get up! What are you still doing in bed?" in my dream. And I opened my eyes and saw him in my doorway with his face half covered in shaving cream and a razor in his hand.

I have a note in my pocket in case I have to sign in at the office, but I dash out of Baba's car and sprint to class right before the bell rings. I'm hot and out of breath, but at least I'm not tardy. Adam looks up as I burst into the room. I haven't seen him since he skipped practice because we didn't have a game scheduled this weekend.

"Hey," I say casually as I pass him on the way to my desk.

"Hey," he replies. I figure things are back to normal, until we line up at lunchtime to go to the cafeteria.

"How come you missed practice?" I ask him. "Were you sick or something?"

"I went to practice with Antonio's team."

"You what?"

"They need a few more players, so Antonio said I could come by and practice with them."

"But the season already started!"

"It's still early enough."

"So what, you're going to play football now?" I say it like I can't believe what I'm hearing. Which I can't.

"Thinking about it." Adam looks at me like he expects me to challenge him. But I don't. We're in the cafeteria now. In my rush to get out of the house this morning, I left my lunch sitting on the counter. I don't say anything else to Adam and stand in line to get a grilled cheese.

Adam heads over to our table and takes a seat with Blake and Keanu. I grab my food and go sit in the spot they've left for me.

"So are you quitting our team, then?" I ask now that we're surrounded by our friends. I know they are going to be as confused as I am.

"Quitting? What are you talking about?" Blake looks at Adam with alarm.

"Why would you quit?" Keanu asks. "Aren't you the star of your team?"

Adam doesn't answer and takes a bite of his sandwich.

"Seriously, dude." Blake presses him. "Why would you quit? We need you."

"He wants to play football," I volunteer.

"I don't know yet," Adam finally says. "I can't do both. The football team practices on the same day twice a week."

"You're going to pick basketball, right? You're team captain," Blake insists. I'm glad he's saying the things I'm thinking. That way I don't have to.

"I don't know. I did awesome at the practice I went to. I love football. And my dad played in high school, so he's excited about it."

"But what about us?" Blake asks.

Exactly. Or more specifically, "What about *me*?" I'm the one who Adam encouraged to try out for his team. I'm the one who worked hard to make it, even when that meant getting grounded in the process. I'm the one who Adam carpools with to games and practices and has fun with. And, oh yeah. I'm also supposed to be his *best friend*.

We stare at him and wait for him to speak. I wonder if he's going to say that basketball isn't as much fun as it was last season. Or that our team isn't as good as it was before. Or that we aren't winning. Because that's got to be why he's doing this, right?

"I'm still friends with you guys even if I play football," Adam finally says. And then he picks up his sandwich again and takes a huge bite.

Blake seems cool with that answer. But I can't help but wonder if Adam even means it, or what's really going to happen. I'm not okay with the way Adam's acting or that he's thinking about quitting our team. But I've learned that chasing the bus doesn't work, and

I'm not chasing Adam, either, or begging him to stay on the team with me. I spend the rest of lunch trying to convince myself that if he doesn't want to play with me, I don't want to play with him. Even if I still do.

13

"Zayd, get up. You need to eat breakfast and get ready for your game." Baba sticks his head through my doorway. I don't move and pull the covers over my head instead. A few minutes later he's back.

"Zayd! Come on, buddy. Time to get up. It's

almost ten. What's up with you this week?"

I roll over and stare at the light on the ceiling. My stomach starts to churn. Am I hungry, or is it fear?

"What's the matter? You feeling okay?" Baba comes into my room and sits on the edge of the bed. He starts to poke me.

"My stomach hurts," I mumble.

"Nervous about the game?" he asks as he tickles my feet. My family knows that my stomach hurts when I'm anxious about something. At least I don't have to keep a food journal anymore like when Mama tried to figure out if I was allergic to something.

"A little," I confess.

"What do you have to be nervous about? You'll do great." I know Baba is trying to encourage me. How do I explain what I'm nervous about? This is our third game of the season and we are 0–2. Coach Wheeler is planning to put me in at point guard. I've only had a week to practice in this position, and I don't feel good about it. People tend to blame the point guard if you don't win. What if I play worse than Adam, which I probably will?

"Coach has me playing point," I say. "And Adam isn't playing."

"Why not?

"He didn't come to practice this week. He's trying out for football instead."

"That's a shame."

"Yeah. We need him."

Baba looks at me for a second, and then he yanks off my covers.

"Well, the team has other good players. Including you."

"I'm not as good as Adam," I argue.

"You're not going to get any better lying in bed. And if Adam's not there, don't you think your team needs you more than ever?"

"I guess so." I never thought of that.

"Then get up. Coach Wheeler will have a fit if you're late."

When I get dressed and go downstairs, Mama is in the kitchen and has some fruit, yogurt, and granola out.

"Something light to get you moving. Want a smoothie?" she offers.

"No thanks. Who's coming to my game?"

"Just Baba today, sweetie. I have to take Zara to Alison's party. Is that okay?"

"Yeah. Totally." She has no idea how okay it is. I don't want anyone watching me today.

Baba and I pull up at the middle school where our game is being held. I see the other team warming up and feel my stomach turn again. They are so big they could be seventh graders, not fourth graders. I could swear one of them has a mustache. They aren't wearing T-shirts underneath their jerseys, and I can see their muscles flexing. Plus, they clearly know their way around a basketball court.

We warm up for a few minutes, and Coach confirms that he's starting me at point. I know I should be excited. I get to START on the team

I've been dying to be on. But as the seconds tick down to tip-off, my heart starts to beat faster, and I get the sensation that I need to use the bathroom even though I don't. I take a look at the other team's starting lineup. Their center must be at least six feet tall.

The whistle blows, and Matthew gets the ball and passes it to me. I dribble up the court and try not to think too much about what's happening.

All of a sudden the kid who is covering me starts to swipe at the ball as I dribble. I'm forced to stop and look for someone to pass to. Then the kid grabs on to the ball and tries to wrestle it away from me.

The whistle blows. "Jump ball," the ref calls.

This time the other team gets the ball. I run back on defense, and then, as a kid goes up for a shot, I get elbowed in the head.

The ref blows the whistle again.

"You okay?" he asks.

I shake my head no, and Coach Wheeler puts in a sub. On my way to the bench I look at the clock. Only forty-six seconds have passed.

I usually feel restless when I'm on the bench, ready to get back in the game and play again. Today I'm happy to sit out for as long as I can. If there were covers on the bench, I'd pull them over my head and pretend to be asleep when Coach asks me to go back in. I'm not ready to be point guard. And as we deal with another humiliating loss, I wonder if maybe Adam has the right idea after all.

14

I pound the ball on the driveway, working my dribble behind the back, between my legs, and with my left hand. I work on keeping it low to the ground like Coach says we should. It's starting to get a little dark outside, and the lamp is on in the family room. I can see my family through the window, having another wedding planning session with my grandparents and Jamal Mamoo.

This time I didn't even bother to ask mamoo if he wanted to play one-on-one. I slipped outside after we ate dinner and started to play by myself. So I'm surprised when the garage door opens and mamoo comes out.

"Leaving?" I ask mid-shot. The ball hits the rim, and mamoo grabs the rebound and puts it back.

"Not yet. What are you doing?"

It's weird when adults ask questions that make no sense. Can't he see exactly what I'm doing? I'm guessing he wants me to say something. I don't. Instead, I keep working on my dribbling. Mamoo was never the same as other adults. He always picked playing video games or basketball with me over sitting around with my parents. And we always had a blast when he did weird voices and told the best jokes ever. We'd crack up until our sides ached. But now it's only about Nadia Auntie and this wedding, all the time.

"How was your game today?" mamoo asks when I don't say anything. He holds out his hands, and I toss the ball to him. Or more like chuck it at him. Hard.

"Fine."

"That's not what I heard." Mamoo laughs a little. "I heard it was brutal."

"Who said that?" I ask.

"Your dad."

"Oh."

"He said you were playing point?"

"Yeah."

Mamoo doesn't say anything for a couple of minutes. He stands there and watches me dribble and take a few free throws.

"That's new. Want to play H-O-R-S-E?" he finally says.

"I'm good," I reply, still dribbling.

"You sure?"

"Don't you have wedding planning to do? Or Nadia Auntie to talk to?" I ask.

"Ah. Got it. So that's what's eating you?"

"No."

"Look, Zayd." Mamoo grabs the ball from me and cradles it in his arm. I'm forced to stop and look at him. "I know I've been . . . um, busy recently. But we're still close and always will be. You know that, right?"

"I don't know." Everyone's been acting strange lately. First Adam, and now mamoo.

"Well, we are. And I can't get through this stuff on my own. Did you hear those ladies in there? They are going to drive me nuts. I can't even think straight, and this wedding planning is just starting." Mamoo starts to dribble the ball, hitting it harder against the pavement than he needs to.

"You're the one who wants to get married," I remind him. "Right?"

"Right. I do." Mamoo pauses his dribbling. "You know, you're the one who got me to start talking to Nadia the first day we met, remember? I owe this entire wedding to you."

"No way, Mamoo. This isn't my fault."

Mamoo starts to chuckle a little. I'm not sure what he's finding funny. I hold out my hands, and mamoo throws the ball back to me. And I start working on my crossover. Alone.

Mamoo watches me for a minute and then starts to walk back into the garage. He stops and turns around after a second.

"So are we good, or do I have to tickle you

and make you pee your pants again?" he asks.

"Yeah," I say. I try not to smile as I remember the time he did that.

I wait to see if he tries to play again, but he turns back around and goes inside. I keep playing and thinking about what he said until it's too dark to see the rim.

15

As far as older siblings go, Zara isn't the absolute worst. I've seen some of my friends' older brothers and sisters, and they are pure evil. Sure, Zara can be a know-it-all a lot. And she tattles. But she also plays basketball with me, tries to be helpful, and can be pretty cool when she wants to be. Her friends are another story. I *hate* it when her friends come over, because when they're around, Zara gets meaner to me. She puts on a show for them or, as Naano says, becomes a "show-off."

Today she has not one, not two, but SIX of her friends coming over for an afternoon "spa day." That's what she decided she wanted to do for her thirteenth birthday party. She passed on bowling. Or a bounce place. Or laser tag. Or anything that sounded exciting. Instead, she wants her friends to come over and paint their nails and watch cheesy movies. When I ask Baba about it, he clutches his heart as if he's in pain.

"I'm going to have a teenage daughter on my hands. God help me," he says with a groan.

"Why do they have to come here? Why don't they go to the mall or literally anywhere else?"

"Well this saves a lot of money. I don't mind," Baba says. "It's only a few hours."

Mama, on the other hand, is loving everything about spa day.

"What is *that*?" I ask when I see her mixing up some kind of concoction in the kitchen.

"Cucumber-mint water," she says proudly. "It's very spa-like." I don't see what's special about a jug of water with slices of cucumber and mint leaves floating in it.

"Is it like lemonade?" I wrinkle up my nose.

"Try it." Mama pours a little into a cup and hands it to me.

"Bleh." I spit it into the sink. It takes like the watery part of a cucumber. "This is gross!"

"Well luckily, it's not for you. You and Adam can drink water. Or apple juice."

"Adam?"

"Yeah, his mom texted. She has a work

emergency and needs to drop him off here for a couple hours."

"Really?"

"Yes, but listen, Zayd." Mama turns around and gives me a stern look. "No bothering the girls, okay? This is an important day for Zara, and I don't want you to ruin it in any way."

"What? Me?" I act insulted.

"Just let them do their thing, okay?"

"Fine with me. They can paint their nails blue and drink cucumbers all they want." I'm relieved to hear that Adam is coming over. We haven't hung out in ages.

The doorbell rings, and both Zara and I run to the door. It's Alison, holding a glittery gift bag.

"Happy birthday, Zara!" she squeals, even though Zara's birthday isn't actually until Wednesday.

Fifteen minutes later the doorbell rings again, and it's another friend. And then another comes. And then finally it's Adam. He looks confused when he arrives and sees a bunch of shoes in the doorway.

"What's going on?" he asks. "Who's here?"

"Zara's having a weird birthday party," I explain. "Let's go to my room."

We walk up the stairs, and just then someone comes out of the bathroom. It's Alison, with globs of greenish-gray slime all over her face.

"AHHH! It's a zombie!" Adam yells.

"AHHH," I join in.

And then we run downstairs into the family room screaming. When we get there, there is sappy violin music playing and even more girls with gunk on their faces. Except these are lying on the carpet with slices of cucumbers where their eyes are supposed to be. It's not enough to drink cucumbers? They have to *wear* them too? Disgusting.

"There's JUST SO MANY OF THEM!" Adam starts to yell. We can't keep a straight face anymore and start laughing hysterically.

One of the masked people sits up suddenly. The cucumbers tumble off her face.

"Mom!" It's Zara. "Can you make these dorks leave? This is NOT relaxing!"

"Zayd!" Mama marches into the room. "I thought I asked you not to bother the girls."

"Adam started it," I say.

"Please, boys?" Mama begs.

"Yeah. Get out," Zara whines.

We leave, just because Mama asked nicely and because I agreed not to ruin Zara's party. And because I want to get to the basement to play video games before the girls try to claim the TV.

16

"Wanna play 2K?" I ask Adam. Then I suddenly remember his new love for football. "Or I guess Madden?"

"2K's cool."

We settle into the old sofa, and Adam asks me about yesterday's game.

"It was awful," I said. "Pretty much the same as the first two weeks." I pause. "Coach put me in at point. It was his idea."

"How'd you do?" Adam asks.

"Terrible. I turned the ball over a lot. We were pressed again."

"That stinks."

"You decide on a team?" I ask.

"Warriors." Adam selects Golden State as his team, and I of course pick Washington.

"No, I mean in real life. Are you going to do basketball or football?"

Adam hits pause and fiddles with the controller.

"I want to stick with football," he says. "But I don't want people to think I'm a quitter. Or that it's because our team is bad."

"Isn't it?"

"No. I mean it's no fun to lose. But I want

to see if I can play football. And I don't know when else I'll have a chance like this, to be on a team with people I know."

"What if you don't want to stick with football?"

"Then maybe I can come back and get my position back." Adam laughs. He starts our game again.

"That probably won't be too hard." I sigh as Adam makes a sweet three-point shot with Steph Curry.

"Don't underestimate yourself," Adam says. "You're better than you think. You always have been."

"No I haven't."

"Coach wouldn't have picked you for the team otherwise."

"I don't have your handles."

"See? There you go again."

I press a button, and John Wall makes an amazing pass to Marcin Gortat, who dunks it right over Kevin Durant.

"In your face!" I cheer.

"That's what you're best at," Adam says. "You're a good playmaker."

"Yeah, in 2K."

"In real life too. I bet Coach noticed your passing. And you always know where each player is on the court."

"You think?"

"Yeah."

"Thanks, man." It's a relief to know that Adam isn't leaving basketball because of me or how bad our team is. And that he might come back some time. Best of all, he thinks I have what it takes to be on point. He was right about me making the team in the first place. I hope he's right about this, too.

"Yeah, no problem. I just hope I play well on the football team." Adam actually sounds nervous, which makes me look up at him in surprise.

"You're awesome at everything you do," I say. Suddenly I realize that Adam never wanted me to feel bad because he's going after what he wants. And I don't anymore. He should have the chance to play the sport he wants, even if it isn't what I want.

"Except for 2K," I add as I dunk on him again. "I'm a beast. Prepare to lose."

17

"I need your help, guys," Mama says. "We need to get Naano's house ready for the weekend."

"What for?" Zara asks. "What's happening this weekend?"

"Naano invited Nadia Auntie's family to come over to finalize plans for the engagement party and start talking about wedding dates," Mama explains. "Now she's panicking about fixing the yard and taking out the good china and stuff. She can't do it alone."

"Isn't the yard Nana Abu's thing?" I ask. My grandfather loves plants. I can picture him spending hours outside with his tools and coming into the house with his pants covered in dirt.

"His knees hurt him too much now, and he shouldn't be doing any heavy lifting at his age. Come on, we only have a couple hours before it gets dark."

We pull up in front of my grandparents' house, and I notice for the first time that the front garden is a total mess. There are buckets of dead plants around the front door, tools scattered in the mulch, and at least three garden hoses jumbled up. When did this happen?

Naano answers the door.

"Asalaamualaikum," she says. "Ah, you brought my skinny mouse and my strong girl. You two going to work?"

"Yes, Naano," we both say.

"Zara, you help Naano with getting out the dishes. Zayd, you're with me out here," Mama orders. She opens up the trunk of her car and pulls out two pairs of gardening gloves, some yard-waste bags, and a broom and rake.

"I feel bad that I let it go this long," Mama says. "We should have come earlier to help out. Not only because people are coming over."

We spend the next hour digging out the dead plants, hauling away the old containers and tools, and sweeping off the front porch. It looks a lot better when we're done.

"Doesn't that feel good?" Mama says, wiping her hair out of her face with her arm.

"What?" I ask.

"Working with your hands," she says. "Seeing the fruits of your labor."

"I guess so," I say, although I'd rather work on my dribble, and we don't actually have any fruit.

We head inside, and Nana Abu is watching cricket in his favorite armchair in the family room. The volume is turned up super loud, blasting an announcer in a British accent.

"Terrific over," the voice says, although he pronounces "over" as "oh-vah."

"Not for us. Too many runs in that over," Nana Abu grumbles. Then he spots me, and his face lights up.

"Zayd, come watch with me," he says.

"Salaams, Abu," Mama says. "Zayd's here to work today. We're getting ready for the Qureshis' visit."

"They're coming here?" Nana Abu asks. "When?"

"This weekend," Mama says. "Don't you remember we were talking about it?"

"Did we?" Nana Abu smiles. "How nice. We will make sure we host them well. What should I do? I can get down those boxes from the garage that your mother uses."

Mama hesitates, and then she points at me.

"Actually why don't you keep Zayd out of trouble while I help Ammi and Zara in the kitchen," she suggests.

"But you . . ." I start to say that she just said I was here to work, but Mama shakes her head slightly.

"It's okay," she murmurs out of the side of her mouth. "Keep Nana Abu company."

SCORE! I get out of doing anything else!

Watching cricket with my grandfather is

one of my favorite things to do. When I was younger, I didn't understand this sport at all. And Nana Abu didn't explain the rules very well, so I had to figure out what an "over" and a "wicket" were on my own. I didn't understand why the batsmen hold their bats pointing downward. Or why the pitches bounce. And most of all I didn't understand why a game could easily last an entire day. But now I kind of get it, and Nana Abu and I can spend hours yelling at the TV together.

Today as we watch, I notice for the first time how the team captain is really the leader on the field.

"Is he telling them where to go?" I ask Nana Abu.

"Yes. Captain tells the players where to be when they are bowling."

"And does he get to pick who bowls?"

"Of course!"

I can't help but think about how easy this guy makes it look to be in charge. Why can't I be that way? My game is coming up, and I need to find a way to be the one to make a difference.

18

It's game day, and the entire gold team, minus Adam, is sitting in a section of the bleachers. Coach Wheeler ordered us to get there half an hour before game time, and it worked.

"If you wander in ten minutes before the

game, you don't play in the first half," he warned us at practice.

The game before ours hasn't ended yet. We sit and wait for them to clear the court so we can warm up. Coach Wheeler comes over to give us a pregame chat. It's the usual pep-talk kind of stuff. Then he points at me.

"Zayd, you're starting on point. You good with that?"

"Yes, Coach!" I reply as I feel myself start to sweat.

"Good." Coach assigns the rest of the positions. "We're playing the Laurel Lightning. They're good, but they are beatable."

The other game finally ends, and we warm up. As I shoot around, I tell myself the things Coach and Adam have said to me over the past week: "Be aggressive. Don't rush shots. Don't pass when you can drive."

Jamal Mamoo is at the game with my family. I guess he wants to show me that we're still boys, or prove to Mama that he can get somewhere by noon on a Saturday. Either way, I'm glad he's here, and I can hear his loud clapping and screaming "LET'S GO, GOLD TEAM!" over all the talking and cheering.

The ref blows the whistle. It's go time. We huddle up, and Coach asks, "Who wants to take us home?"

This time I don't hesitate, and I put my arm into the middle. "One, two, three, MD HOOPS!" We walk out onto the court, and tip-off goes our way. Blake passes me the ball, and I dribble up the court. There's no press, and I'm able to run the four-out play that Coach likes. *SWISH!* Sam makes an easy bucket. We're off to a good start!

We run back on defense, and Ravindu gets

a steal and makes a layup off a fast break. Our side of the bleachers goes nuts, as if we are in the NBA finals, not the first minute of our fourth game of the season.

"Nice shot!" I yell to Ravindu.

The next possession the Lightning throw the ball out of bounds, and it comes back to us. This time as I take the ball up, they start to double-team me, but I get the ball away in time. We pass the ball around the perimeter until Matthew drives inside and takes a shot. It bounces off the rim, and I grab it, pump fake, and put it back in.

"WOOO-HOOO!" I hear Jamal Mamoo.

We're up 6–0, and we look good. The entire team seems as determined as I am today to get the job done. The Lightning score on their next possession, and we keep going back and forth. We have some good plays and lose the ball a couple of times. They airball a shot and give it back to us for an easy two points.

Coach puts in subs, and I head to the bench and pick up my water bottle.

"I like the toughness," he says to us. "Good control, Zayd." He nods at me.

I look into the stands, and Zara raises her fist. And the rest of my family is grinning like they won the lottery. It's not even halftime, and we're only up by six. But this is the best we've looked the whole season.

Before I know it, halftime is over, and we're back to the starting lineup for the second half. The Lightning get the ball, and we press them, but they manage to get a shot off and it's good.

"That's all right. Get back," I hear Coach yell. Blake inbounds to me, and I take the ball down, looking for an open pass. Blake sets a

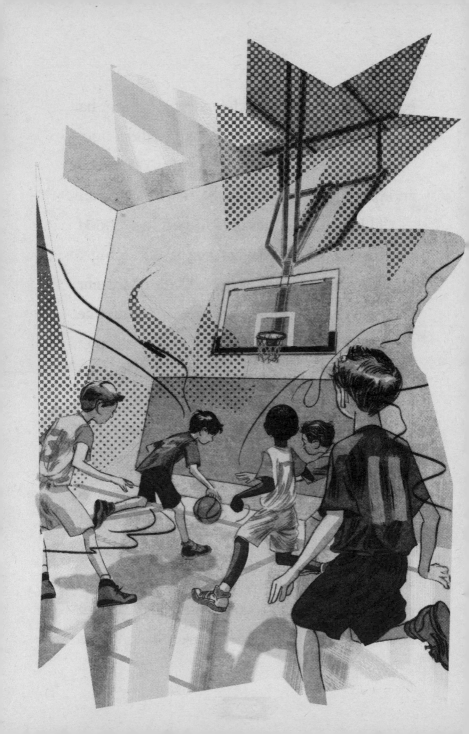

screen and stuffs the defender. I get the ball back and see a wide-open lane to the hoop, but also Sam waiting on the wing. I pause for a second, fighting the urge to pass the ball. Then I drive to the hoop and pull up. *SWISH!*

In that moment whatever I was doing to psych myself out disappears. I finally get what it takes to be a good point guard. Sometimes you're there to move the ball. Sometimes you're there to see the open man and get him the ball or take the defense by surprise by driving when they expect you to pass. Getting to be a leader, and to do it all, is the beauty of being the point guard, and why it's my favorite position to see in action. I don't only love watching John Wall. Now I now can try to play like him too. If I'm even a tenth as good, I'll be incredible.

Everyone is hot today. Blake gets an amazing shot and one. Sam gets what I'm convinced is a three-pointer, even though the ref gave him two. Ravindu has three steals. And I have three assists, six points, and only one turnover. We manage to pull out our first victory of the season. And even though I miss Adam, it still feels amazing. A tiny part of me wonders if it's even better than it would have been with him. That's because now, I'm finally on point.

19

"We have a very good friend who is a doctor in Richmond. He wants to say a few words. Maybe a dua. Or a short ghazl," Nadia Auntie's father says.

Nadia Auntie and Jamal Mamoo look at each other in alarm.

"Abu, we were thinking of no speeches other than the emcee, the imam, and our parents . . . if you feel compelled to say something," Nadia Auntie says.

"No, no," Uncle Qureshi continues. "Dr. Rana always speaks at weddings. He will mind if we don't ask him."

"So the menu is set?" Nadia's mother asks. "Did you pick the caterer?"

"Not yet," Nadia Auntie answers. "We're still working on it."

Naano mutters something in Urdu, but I hear the words "southern shmuthern," and the elders start to chuckle.

Jamal Mamoo turns red.

We're sitting in Naano's living room, in a house that I've never seen this tidy. The stacks of Nana Abu's books and newspapers are put away. There's no pile of medicines or jumbo-size packages of fiber-drink powder on the counter in the kitchen.

We've finished a delicious dinner that Mama and Naano spent three days cooking. And now the wedding planning is happening over chai, fruit, cheesecake, and a variety of mithai that the Qureshis brought over on a fancy silver tray.

"What about the date? It is not good to delay. Why can't we do April?" Naano says.

Nadia Auntie's mom nods in agreement.

"I have to check the kids' spring break schedule," Mama says.

"April is too soon." Jamal Mamoo finally speaks up. "We were thinking May at the earliest. Or June."

"June is too hot," Naano declares.

"Yes, yes, too hot." Nadia Auntie's mom looks like she wants to high-five Naano they are so in sync about the weather.

Jamal Mamoo starts to sweat as if it's June already. Nadia Auntie excuses herself and goes into the hallway near the bathroom. A couple of minutes later, mamoo gets up and follows her. I wait a minute and then sneak out of the room too.

Nadia Auntie and Jamal Mamoo are hanging in the hallway talking in hushed whispers. Nadia Auntie's eyes are huge and she looks panicked, and my uncle is mopping his forehead with a paper napkin. I feel sorry for him. And even though I know it's rude to interrupt them, I can't help it.

"Can I tell you something, Mamoo?" I ask.

"What is it, Skeletor?" Mamoo turns around halfway.

"Zara got to have a spa party for her birth-day where they lay around with cucumbers on their eyes, even though I get in trouble for wasting food."

"Um, I'm sorry, Zayd. Can we talk about this later?"

"What I mean is, it didn't matter that I wanted her to pick laser tag. Or that Baba wanted her to stay twelve forever."

"What are you trying to say, Zayd?" Nadia Auntie moves closer to me.

"I mean this is your wedding, right? Not anyone else's. We get to pick what to do for our birthdays that happen every year. And this wedding is a once-in-a-lifetime thing, right?"

"Inshallah." Jamal Mamoo smiles at Nadia, and she gives him a little punch in the arm.

"So stop letting Mama and Naano and Nadia's mom boss you around and tell you what to eat and what to wear and who gets to talk."

"We have to respect their wishes too," Jamal Mamoo says. "It's a family event."

"I know. Mama said that the wedding planning was a big team thing. What I'm saying is you guys need to run point. Let everyone else play and help out. But you have to call the shots. Or else everything is going to stay a big mess like this."

Jamal Mamoo and Nadia Auntie look at each other, and then they smile.

"We're being schooled by a fourth grader, using basketball terms," Nadia Auntie says. "You're totally right, Zayd. I've been too stressed out by all this and not having any fun."

"Me neither," Jamal Mamoo agrees. "I feel pulled in so many directions, and what we want is getting lost."

"So go back in there and be a boss," I say, giving the two of them a gentle shove back toward the living room. "I'm telling you. Trust me."

I didn't do the best job explaining it to them, but I think they got my point. Because if there's one thing I've realized, it's that everyone should have the chance to go after their dreams. Whether it's making a birthday wish with green slime on your face, putting together a wedding that includes what the bride and groom want, trying out a new sport, or stepping up, finding your groove, and turning a losing team around.

"I got this, Skeletor," Jamal Mamoo says as we walk back into the living room. "When did you get so smart all of a sudden?"

"Very funny." I stick my tongue out.

Mamoo puts his arm around me, and somehow that turns into a headlock. I punch him and wiggle out of his grip, and he lets out his wacky laugh. Nadia Auntie and I look at each other and crack up too. As I laugh, I know something for sure. Just like mamoo is going to finally be captain of his wedding team, I'm going to be the next captain of the gold team. And with us in charge, we'll be winners no matter what.

BOUNCE BACK

For Humza
—*H. K.*

To Ryan and Lizzie
—*S. W. C.*

ACKNOWLEDGMENTS

As I wrote the third book in this series, I thought a lot about how lucky I am to have such an amazing team around me. I can't thank my editor, Zareen Jaffery; agent, Matthew Elblonk; and members of my writing group—Laura Gehl, Ann McCallum, and Joan Waites— enough for helping me shape this series and bring it to life. I'm also carried by the love of librarians, educators, and fellow writers who make me believe I can do this. Thank you to each and every one of you who has shared my books with a reader, said an encouraging word to me, or made a comment or suggestion that has helped keep me going. A special shout-out to my home team: Edie Ching, Jacqueline Jules, Susan Kusel, Karen Leggett, Kathie Meizner, Kathie Weinberg, and the other wonderful members of the Children's Book Guild of D.C. for being with me over the years and pushing me forward.

Some of the very best things about being an author are getting to talk to incredible kids across the country and globe, receiving letters from them, and hearing that they value what I do. There's no better feeling. Thank you to all of you who I have met, or haven't yet, for reading and making my books part of your lives. I'm grateful to the biggest basketball fans and most valuable players in my life, my sons, Bilal and Humza, who worked with to me to brainstorm ideas, check terms, design plays, and create a winning story line. For this book, I also had my friend Mikail Mirza share his basketball knowledge and creativity when I was struggling to figure it out, along with the enthusiastic support of Zara and Isa

Mirza. My young friend Zayd Salahuddin lent me his first name, along with Musa, Yusuf, Rabiya, Sumaiya, Rania, Suleiman, Adam, and the other special kids in my life who have been so wonderful in sharing their ideas and excitement with me over the years. I remain forever indebted to my parents and family for their endless love, patience, and support. And to my husband, Farrukh—you inspired this series, and continue to inspire me.

1

My new basketball hoop is going to be amazing. I waited forever to finally replace the rusted, bent rim I've been playing on for the past four years. This one has a clear shatterproof backboard like the ones in the NBA. Plus, there's an adjustable height lever you can use with one hand. I chipped in for half of it using the money I had saved up from my birthday and Eid. My parents paid for the rest.

But after three hours and thirty-seven minutes the hoop is still in pieces all over the driveway. My dad is drenched in sweat. My uncle, Jamal Mamoo, is cursing under his breath and probably wishing he hadn't come over today. And I think my mother is pretending to understand Chinese, since that's the only language in the instruction booklet. She keeps rotating the pages to look at the drawings from different angles.

"I think it's the other end that's supposed to go in this thingy," Mama says, pointing at the booklet.

"No. It. Doesn't. Fit. That. Way." Baba has a washer pressed between his lips and speaks through it in a low growl.

"It's too hot outside," Naano declares from the doorway of the garage. My grandmother doesn't believe humans should be in the sun for more than five minutes. "How many hours are you going to do this? Stop now. Come have chai."

I look around in alarm, but no one seems ready to quit yet. My family is the kind that loves to watch do-it-yourself shows together on TV. These are the programs about regular people who tear out their kitchen cabinets or showers and install shiny new ones. We comment on their choices and how all the people seem just like us. Until they start cutting tiles or using power tools. Then we decide they must secretly be professionals.

The do-it-yourselfers on TV are nothing like the Saleem family. We don't usually fix or build anything ourselves. My parents don't own a toolbox or a single leather tool belt. There's only a sagging shelf in the corner of the garage that holds a hammer, a box of nails, random hooks, and a screwdriver or two.

But it cost an extra seventy-nine dollars to get the hoop assembled. So here we are, putting on a bad reality show for our neighbors. I can't prove it, but it sure feels like they are walking their dogs a lot more than usual today and smiling at us extra hard.

"You guys are doing it wrong." My older sister, Zara, saunters outside holding a glass of lemonade and wearing a know-it-all look on her face.

"Zara!" Mama snaps her head up from the drawings. "We don't need your commentary right now."

"Okay. I thought you'd want to know I watched a video with instructions. The guy was NOT doing that."

"Wait." Baba turns around and glares at Mama. "There's a video?"

"There's no video listed on here," Mama says, flipping over the booklet. "Unless the link is written in Chinese?"

"What video?" I ask Zara.

"The one on YouTube. There's a guy who goes through all the steps one at a time for this exact model basketball hoop. You should watch it."

"YOU THINK?" Baba explodes. The lady from two doors down and her tiny yappy dog both jump up, startled as he shouts. I can't help but grin.

Jamal Mamoo catches my eye, drops the pieces of the base he was fumbling to put together, and lets out his wacky laugh. Soon Mama joins in too. Before we know it, we're all howling with laughter. Even Baba. Nana Abu, my grandfather, comes shuffling outside because of all the commotion.

"Hold on a second." Mama puts up a hand, gasping for air. "What's so funny?"

Her question just makes us all laugh harder. I drop to the grass and roll around until my stomach hurts, but in a good way.

Two hours and twenty-three more minutes later, I finally get to try out my Spalding hoop. It's as nice as I thought it would be. Maybe nicer. Best of all, we did it ourselves. Mostly. The dog lady felt sorry for us and brought over her husband and his set of tools to help us. Zara brought out her tablet and kept rewinding the parts of the video until we figured it all out. Nana Abu stepped in for Jamal Mamoo when he left to meet his fiancée, Nadia Auntie, for a wedding-cake tasting. (I volunteered for the tasting job, but my uncle said no way.)

I take a couple of shots and watch them go off the shiny new backboard into the perfectly straight rim. My game is already so much better than it was last year. I'm starting point guard on the team I've worked so hard to be a part of. I'm hoping Coach Wheeler will pick me to be our new team captain now that my best friend Adam left. We've turned our season around and have a chance to make the playoffs. Plus now I can practice at home and not worry about adjusting my shot to make it go in.

"We did it," Baba says. He puts his arm around Mama, and they gaze at the hoop proudly. They're going to have a lot more to be proud of soon. I can only imagine incredible things ahead of me. My future is looking as good as my new hoop.

It's extra hot in the gym where we practice. The air conditioner isn't working, and the air feels thick and heavy. Plus Coach Wheeler is running us hard. We did the eleven-man fast-break drill, and I was on defense with Blake. The two of us were trying to stop three people from scoring. I can feel sweat dripping down my back.

"Okay, water break," Coach yells. "Make it quick."

"It's so hot," Blake whines to me. "I'm dying. It's hotter in here than it is outside."

"Yeah," I mumble. It takes too much energy to complain. I glance at the clock. Fifteen more minutes until the end of practice. I'm working up the nerve to talk to Coach about the team captain opening. I'll have to make it quick. It's Thursday, so Naano is going to pick me up since Zara has volleyball, and she hates to wait. Maybe I can get her to take me to Carmen's for some Italian ice. The idea of the delicious fruity ice that tastes like a frozen Jolly Rancher makes me feel cooler already.

"Next up is the warrior drill," Coach says. "Let's give it our all until the end of practice, guys."

The warrior drill is one of my favorites. It's

basically a rebounding-and-put-back battle. A few guys are on the perimeter, and three of us are on the inside. The perimeter players take turns shooting. Those of us on the inside fight one another for the rebound and have to put it back for a score twice before we can get out.

I'm on the inside with Sam and Matthew, and Blake takes a shot from the three-point line. I try to box out Sam. We both jump up.

SWISH!

Blake makes the shot instead of hitting the rim. We turn around and look at him.

"Oops!" He shrugs as if to say he can't help being too good to miss.

"Show off!" Sam mutters.

"Nice shot." Coach nods to Blake. "Come on—let's keep going."

Coach passes Ravindu the ball, and he takes the shot this time and misses. It hits the rim on my side. I've had my legs bent, ready to jump at the perfect moment, and I'm up just as the ball bounces. I grab the ball with both hands and come down hard . . . right onto Matthew's foot.

YOW!

My foot turns in a weird way, and I start to lose my balance. You know how when you start to fall, you actually see yourself moving in slow motion? And there's a moment when you try to stop it from happening? That is exactly what happens to me. Except I can't regain control of my body and put an arm out to break my fall.

THUMP!

I hit the ground hard. The ball pops out and rolls away.

"Hey, man, you okay?" Matthew extends his hand to help me up.

"YEESSHH!" I gasp as a searing pain rips through my ankle.

"Uh-oh. What's the matter?" Matthew looks scared as I grab on to him.

Coach Wheeler comes running over. He puts his arm around my waist.

"Zayd! Be careful. Can you put weight on your foot?"

My heart is racing.

"I don't know," I say.

"It'll be okay. Test it out."

"OW, OW, OW!" I wince as I take a small step, and pain shoots through my ankle up my leg. I have to lift my foot off the floor again.

I feel Coach Wheeler and Matthew look at each other over my head as I stand on my good foot. A lightning bolt of fear runs through me, and I suddenly feel a chill even though I'm drenched in sweat. What did I do to my ankle?

3

The lady sitting behind the counter hands Mama a clipboard and a pen.

"Insurance card and photo ID," she says, not looking up.

"Here you go," Mama says cheerfully. She's always super nice to grumpy people. I think she does it to make them feel bad for not being friendlier.

I'm sitting on a chair in a waiting room at the Rockville Sports Medicine Center, wearing only one of my sneakers. On the other foot I'm wearing a sock. Over that sock, I'm wearing one of Baba's socks, which Mama stuffed with bags of ice.

She had to come pick me up from practice last night instead of Naano. I pretended something was in my eye when I saw her and the tears threatened to flow. Coach helped me into the car, and Zara and Mama both led me into the house. Every time I tried to step on my foot, I had to stifle a yell. I couldn't sleep last night because I kept waking up from the pain whenever I turned over. Mama got me an early appointment with the doctor this morning. So here I am instead of being in school.

"Zayd Saleem," a nurse finally says from a doorway.

"I'll help you," Mama says as I slowly get up. I lean on her and hop over to the nurse, who pats my shoulder.

"Let's see what's going on with you, tough guy. Come this way."

We head into a tiny examining room holding a bed and a couple of chairs. The nurse asks me a bunch of questions, takes my temperature and blood pressure, and clips something onto my finger. It's too much work to get on the scale, and I'm still wearing the homemade ice pack, so we estimate my weight. Finally the doctor comes in, wearing a white coat and big smile.

"I'm Dr. Alam. Nice to meet you," he says, shaking my hand. "What happened?"

"I jumped for a rebound and landed on

my friend's foot and hurt my ankle."

"I see. Basketball player, huh? Rough sport for ankles and knees. Although it keeps me in business." He winks at Mama, and she smiles to appreciate his joke. I don't.

Dr. Alam kneels down and gently unwraps the ice from my foot. He presses in a few spots and rotates my foot slowly.

"OW!"

Frowning, the doctor asks me about my pain level. He points to a chart highlighting a row of cartoon faces. There's a regular yellow smiley face on one end and a bright red crying face on the other. I point to the number seven face: It's pretty upset, but not crying or anything.

"Hmm," Dr. Alam types some notes. "I'm going to need a quick X-ray to check for a fracture."

"FRACTURE?" I sit up straight, and my heart starts to pound faster.

"Don't worry. We'll get you fixed up so you can get back on the court."

The court. My heart still races as I think about how I need to get back to it . . . and quick. There are only a few weeks left in the regular season before playoffs, and I can't afford to be injured. My stomach starts to hurt, so I try to push those thoughts out of my mind and focus on the X-ray machine. It's actually kind of cool to see my leg bones glowing on the screen. They remind me of Jamal Mamoo's nickname for me, Skeletor, which he says is because I'm bony.

When we get back to the exam room, Dr. Alam points to the X-ray images on his computer.

"Good news. There's no fracture."

"Oh thank God," Mama says. She lets out a big sigh, and I see her mouthing a prayer.

Dr. Alam moves toward a drawing of a leg on the wall. "You have what we call a high ankle sprain, Zayd. It's a bit more serious than a regular sprain. That's why you have pain here, in these ligaments."

He says some other things, but I stop listening. My mind is fixated on one thing.

"When can I play basketball again?" I ask.

"I'm hoping in about four weeks, depending on how well you do."

"FOUR WEEKS?" I'm louder than I meant

to be, and Mama shushes me. I keep talking anyway. "We still have games left in our season and need to win to get into the playoffs! I HAVE to play!"

"Sorry, buddy, you need to stay off it as much as possible." Dr. Alam looks at my face and smiles gently. "Tell you what. Come back in two weeks, and we'll reassess."

"Does he need crutches?" Mama asks.

"For the first couple weeks," Dr. Alam says. As they continue to speak, my heart sinks into my stomach. I've always wanted to hop around on crutches. It looks like so much fun. But today, they're the last things in the world I want. All season I've dreamed of taking my team to the playoffs. I don't know how I'm supposed to do that now.

4

Mama dumps a bunch of little bags onto the kitchen table. Everyone is drinking chai and eating Naano's favorite biscuits, which she pronounces "bizcoot."

"What about this one? Isn't it cute?" Mama's holding a small, sparkly gold pouch that has a red drawstring on top. I can imagine a tiny pirate using it to stash even tinier gold coins.

"How about this plain one?" Dad picks up a bag made out of a gauzy white fabric. "It's classic."

We all look at him in surprise, and he shrugs.

"What? I'm trying to participate."

"Nadia and I would prefer to use something recycled," Jamal Mamoo says, which causes Naano to snort.

"You want to give people trash? How about empty chips packets?" she says.

"No, Ammi," Jamal Mamoo explains. "We're thinking of little Chinese-take-out-style boxes made out of recycled paper. Nadia found them online."

Mama gives Naano a look I can tell means "Let it go."

Ever since I gave Jamal Mamoo and Nadia

Auntie a pep talk about taking control of their wedding, they've taken it, all right. Mamoo has a color-coded list on his laptop for each part of the wedding, including guests, vendors, and menu. There's still some grumbling and arguments, but Naano and Nadia's mom finally agreed to let them plan their own wedding. Mostly.

"What are these bags or boxes even for?" I ask. I'm sitting in the corner, elevating my foot on a stool. I'm wearing the "walking boot" that Dr. Alam gave me along with my crutches. It looks like a giant blue snow boot with the toes cut open and Velcro straps. My crutches are leaning against the wall near me.

"They're the goodie bags for the people who come to the wedding," Zara says. "We'll put them on the tables."

"What do you want inside? Nuts and dried

fruits? Chocolate?" Mama asks. "I vote for chocolate."

I expect Jamal Mamoo to agree. Instead, he shakes his head.

"Fortune cookies." He grins. "We're ordering custom ones with hilarious messages and little sayings about us on the inside."

"OH MY GOSH. THAT'S SO CUTE!" Zara gushes.

Even Naano nods her head in approval. She loves fortune cookies.

"What do you think, Skeletor?" Jamal Mamoo asks me.

"That's cool," I mumble. I feel slightly guilty that I'm not pretending to be more excited. But this wedding is all anyone is talking about, although it's still a month away.

Now I see Jamal Mamoo and Mama exchange a look.

"Come on, man," Jamal Mamoo says. "I need you to cheer up. I can't do this wedding thing without you. You're my best man."

"Yeah, Zayd," Zara chimes in. "You're in charge of the rings. And you have to dance at the mehndi." The pre-wedding party where everyone sings and dances is Zara's department, and she's planning every detail.

"I can't *dance!*" I remind everyone.

"Oh come on. You're not that bad of a dancer. I'll show you the moves. You can stand in the back," Zara says.

"I can't WALK properly!" I shout. "I can't RUN! Or JUMP! How am I supposed to DANCE?"

"Chill out, dude. I'm trying to help." Zara tosses her hair.

I can't help being grumpy. It's only been a couple of days since we saw the doctor, but I don't feel any better yet. Plus, I have basketball practice tomorrow, and Baba said I should still go to support my team despite my injury. If I don't get to play, I think I should at least get to chill at home and watch extra TV.

"You're going to be okay, Zayd." Jamal Mamoo comes over to me, picks up one of my crutches, and uses it to poke me. "Come on. I think we need to take a break from all this wedding stuff and play some 2K."

"Fine."

I know he's trying to cheer me up, as I hop down the stairs and settle into the couch. Naano for sure is trying to make me feel better too when she sends Zara downstairs with a mango milkshake for me a little later. But even after Jamal Mamoo lets me win, and I drain the last drop of my milkshake, I only feel a tiny bit less lousy.

5

"Can I please help Zayd get to the lunchroom safely?" Adam asks Mr. Thomas. It's ten minutes before dismissal, and my best friend is using his extra-serious and responsible voice that he saves for teachers.

"I think he can manage by himself. Don't

you, Zayd?" Mr. Thomas raises his eyebrows at me as I stand up and fumble for my crutches. I have a note from the office giving me permission to leave class early to make my way down the halls before they get crowded. It ends up giving me an extra half hour of free time a day.

Adam pops up from his desk and hands me my crutches. He carefully tucks each one under my arms, and I hold on to the handles.

"I can't carry my lunch." I shrug, looking as helpless as I can.

"All right." Mr. Thomas sighs. "But no horsing around, boys. Head straight to the lunchroom."

"Yes, sir." Adam grins. He grabs my lunch and his own from our cubbies, and we stumble out of the room, bumping into desks, while everyone else stares at us, jealous.

"YES! Freedom!" Adam throws up his hands when we get into the hallway and he shuts the door behind us. "It's so great you're hurt."

I whack him, using one of my crutches.

"Is NOT."

"You know what I mean. Careful with the throwing arm." Adam rubs the side of his arm. Ever since he started playing football instead of basketball with me, he talks as if he's in the NFL or something. "Where should we go?"

"The lunchroom?"

"Let's go to the kindergarten wing. They might have cupcakes or donuts."

"Mr. Thomas said go straight to lunch," I say.

"We are going straight. The long way. Come on!"

The hallway is wide and empty, and I can swing freely on the crutches without bumping into anything.

"You're getting pretty good on those," Adam says.

"Yeah, I guess." I want to complain about how it's not fun at all and how I wish I could walk and play like normal.

"Can I try them?" he asks.

"Now?"

"Yeah. No one will see." Adam puts our lunches on the floor and reaches for the crutches.

"Okay."

I slip off the crutches, hand them to Adam, and lean against the wall. He takes off down the hall, but he's half skipping and using both of his legs.

"You're cheating!" I yell after him. "You need to keep one leg up the way I do."

A door pops open,

and my old kindergarten teacher, Ms. Riley, sticks her head out.

"What are you two doing? Where are you supposed to be?" she says. Her usual cheery face is scowling.

"Going to lunch," Adam pants. "We have a pass. He's hurt."

Ms. Riley looks down at my boot. Then she turns her gaze to Adam holding my crutches.

"That's no excuse for disturbing other classes. Get to the lunchroom before I write you a pink slip."

"Sorry," Adam mumbles.

"Feel better, Zayd," Ms. Riley says. She gives me a sympathetic half smile. We don't get cupcakes, but at least we don't get in trouble, either.

During recess, Adam has the brilliant idea to organize a crutches race. We keep time while

Blake, Chris, Adam, and I take turns hopping on the crutches from one end of the blacktop to the other. Chris is so much taller than me that he has to stoop to use the crutches. Blake is surprisingly quick. And Adam keeps track of everyone's times and whether they beat me.

"You smoked us all!" Adam high-fives me. "You're so fast!"

"That was awesome," Blake adds. "Let's do it again tomorrow."

I agree, and as I head back to class, I notice my crutches are all scratched up from falling on the asphalt so many times. I don't care, though, since I'm counting down the days until I can get rid of them and get back on the court.

6

"How many weeks did you say?" Coach Wheeler is looking at his clipboard at his starting lineup. He's tapping his pen the way he always does when he's thinking.

"Four. So I have three weeks and two days left," I say.

"Sorry to hear it. You in pain?"

"Not much anymore. I'm going to get checked in two weeks, and the doctor said I might be able to play sooner." Did Dr. Alam actually say that? Or am I just wishing he did? I'm not sure.

"We'll miss you. Don't rush it, though. Make sure you heal properly."

I look at Coach in surprise. He's always pushing us so hard, sweating on the sidelines, and yelling during our games. I thought he'd want me back as soon as possible.

"So, um. Who are you going to put in on point?"

"It'll have to be Sam." Coach is frowning at the clipboard.

"Sam?"

"Yeah. I think he'll do all right."

"Um. Okay."

Ravindu comes up behind me.

"Oh man! Did you do that when you fell at practice?"

"Yeah."

"How long are you out?"

"Like three or four weeks."

"That means you miss the rest of the season!"

"Yeah." Ravindu talks too much.

"But we're playing the Lightning again."

The Lightning. We played them twice last season. Their players come to games in training shirts and take them off during warm-ups, the way the Wizards do. The names of their plays, "isolation" and "four out," sound legit. Ours have silly names like "suns" and "horns." A lot of the kids on the Lightning are tall, and they behave as if they're being scouted every game. Their attitude intimidates everyone, and we were scared of them too. Until we finally figured out how to break their press and win last time we played them.

"We need you," Ravindu continues. "We can't beat them without you."

"Thanks," I say. Ravindu is all right.

I sit on the bench and watch my team doing layups. Coach Wheeler pulls Sam aside, and I can tell when he says Sam needs to take my spot. Sam starts to nod his head quickly, and I hear him say "Okay, Coach" as he glances at me a few times.

I suddenly feel hot and sweaty, and my foot starts to itch inside my boot. Grabbing my crutches, I go outside to wait for Mama to pick me up. I'm going to convince Baba that I don't need to be at practice again. I'll come back in three weeks and two days, unless I'm ready to play sooner.

7

"*Ballay ballay!*" everyone shouts.

"*Ballay ballay, bai torr punjaaban di,*" the auntie sitting in the middle of the floor sings loudly. She's banging on the wooden part of a two-sided drum using a spoon. Another lady is playing the drum with her hands.

The room is packed with mostly women and girls. They are crammed around the drummer, clapping and singing songs I don't understand. Nadia Auntie is perched on some bedlike thing draped in colorful fabric.

"Ballay ballay," Zara joins in for the refrain. She's reading the words off a paper and claps every now and then, sitting close to Mama. Naano is seated on a chair on the side next to Nadia Auntie's mom. They smile and nod but aren't singing or clapping. Every few minutes Naano leans over and whispers to Nadia Auntie's mom, and they both giggle. I'm pretty sure Naano is making wisecracks.

We're in the basement of some friends of Nadia Auntie's family, who are hosting a dholki for Jamal Mamoo and Nadia Auntie. When Mama told us about it a few days ago, and explained how a dholki was a pre-mehndi, or a *practice* singing and dancing party, Baba and I exchanged a look of panic.

"Zayd and I don't have to go, right?" he said.

"You should be there to support Jamal," Mama argued. "They would want us all to come."

"I thought dholkis were only for ladies?"

"No. It depends on the host. And they invited everyone."

I could tell Baba knew it was a losing battle when he tried to use me as an excuse.

"What about Zayd's ankle? Shouldn't he be resting it?"

I put on an extra-pained expression to help him out.

"Zayd goes to school and manages. He'll be fine. We're all going."

And that settled it.

Mama picked out matching shalwar kameezes for Baba and me: a deep maroon top over white pants. She tried to get Nana Abu to wear the same thing as us. But when we picked him up, Nana Abu had forgotten and was wearing a black vest over a cream shalwar kameez. He still looked sharp, though. I'd look better if I didn't have to roll up one of my pant legs to wear my walking boot.

Now all the men are sitting upstairs in the living room talking about cricket scores, the Pakistani prime minister, and other stuff so boring it makes my brain hurt. Jamal Mamoo was ordered to arrive later, around dinnertime. I think it's weird he doesn't get to be at a party that's supposed to be for him for the whole time, but Mama said it was so he could make a grand entrance. She told mamoo she'd text him fifteen minutes before he should come. I decided hanging out downstairs was the best option until he gets here.

"Zayd!" An auntie runs into the room and finds me sitting near the stairs. She obviously doesn't notice the giant boot on my foot when she says, "Beta, go run and get your mom. Quickly!"

"What's wrong?" I ask. Her voice is strange.

"Your grandfather. He fainted."

"Is he okay?" I jump up, forgetting my ankle, and feel a shock of pain.

"I see your mom," the auntie says, ignoring me, and she starts to push through the ladies to get to Mama.

Mama gets up and dashes up the stairs, her face white. Zara grabs Naano and follows more slowly. I hop behind them as fast as I can. When I get to the living room, Nana Abu is sitting on a sofa, surrounded by people.

Someone tries to hand him a glass of water, and he shakes his head. Another person is wiping his head using a kitchen towel.

As Naano gets closer, the others move out of the way. When she reaches him, she puts her hand on his shoulder. They speak to each other in Urdu while Baba and Mama huddle together talking with Nadia's dad.

"What's going on?" I pull on Zara's arm.

"I don't know," she says. And we both move closer to our parents.

"We should take him to the hospital," Baba is saying. "He needs to be checked out."

"I agree," Mama says.

My stomach starts to twist and churn when I hear the word "hospital." I hope Nana Abu is going to be okay.

8

The hospital waiting room is small and crowded. I'm sitting next to Jamal Mamoo, and Zara is on his other side. We're both leaning on him.

Jamal Mamoo's wearing the fancy shalwar kameez for the dholki he never went to. Mama called to tell him to meet us at Suburban Hospital when we left. Everyone from the party was ready to follow us to the hospital, but Mama begged them not to come, including Nadia Auntie's family.

"You have all these guests here," she said. "Please stay and enjoy and keep my father in your prayers."

Naano and Mama are in Nana Abu's room, and Baba is pacing the hall. Jamal Mamoo bought us a bunch of chips and candy bars from the vending machine, but no one is interested in eating anything.

"Mamoo?" I interrupt while he's texting Nadia Auntie.

"What's up, Skeletor?"

"What does 'ballay ballay' mean?"

Jamal Mamoo chuckles.

"I have no idea," he admits. "I don't know

what any of those wedding songs are talking about. Even though the aunties love them."

I see Baba talking to a doctor in the hallway, and Jamal Mamoo jumps up to join them. After a few minutes they come back into the waiting room.

"How's Nana Abu?" Zara asks.

"Can he go home now?" I add.

"Not yet," Baba says. "Nana Abu had a . . . ah . . . minor heart attack."

"A . . . HEART . . . ATTACK?" Zara starts to wail.

"No, no, no, it wasn't serious. He's going to be okay. The doctor said it's a warning to take better care of himself." Mamoo rubs her shoulders while Zara tries to pull herself together.

"When can he go home?" I ask. There's a giant lump in my throat.

"He needs to have a small procedure

tomorrow morning. Then he'll be home soon, inshallah," Baba says.

"Can we see him?" Zara asks with a sniffle.

"Sure. He'll be happy to see you. Come on." Baba takes Zara by the hand.

I hesitate.

"Need help, Skeletor?" Jamal Mamoo asks. "Isn't it time to get rid of those crutches?"

"I'm okay," I say. I trail behind them down the hall to where the patient rooms are. Some of the doors are open, and I can see the bottom half of beds and people's feet. It makes my stomach churn again to imagine my grandfather lying there the same way.

"Here we are." Baba pushes open the door to room A32. I see Naano first, sitting on a chair by the bed. She has her scarf on her hair and is praying. A worn copy of the Quran is sitting next to her.

Zara rushes over to Nana Abu, whose eyes grow bigger when he sees us and he gives us a tiny wave. She takes his hand and grasps it inside her own.

"How are you feeling?" she asks in a hushed voice. "Does it hurt?"

"I feel fine," Nana Abu says. "They are taking good care of me here."

I don't move closer. Nana Abu looks so small in the big hospital bed and older than he usually does. He's wearing a hospital gown instead of his nice party outfit, and his gray hair is a mess. A clear tube sticking in his hand is attached to a bag hanging on a pole. A screen above the bed is displaying zigzagged lines. I know one of the lines is his heartbeat because of cartoons. My own heart tightens when I see it.

"Zayd?" Mama asks me. "Don't you want to say salaam to Nana Abu?"

"We're both broken now, eh, Zayd?" Nana Abu says, motioning for me to come closer.

I swallow hard as I inch forward. The lump in my throat is growing bigger. If I try to speak, I'm going to start bawling. Jamal Mamoo is watching me closely, and he suddenly cuts in front of me.

"Abu, you saved me from being forced to dance in front of the aunties," Jamal Mamoo says extra loudly. "But seriously? A heart attack? You could have faked a fever or something."

Nana Abu starts to laugh.

Jamal Mamoo looks around. "I'm starving. Is there any real food in here? Did anyone pack up some food from the party for the handsome groom-to-be?"

Naano looks up from her prayer.

"Did they?" she asks. "I want biryani."

"Me too," Jamal Mamoo agrees. "I'm going to ask Nadia to bring some over right now."

"And some dessert!" Zara adds.

"Can she bring the drum, too?" I pipe up, finally able to speak.

Jamal Mamoo winks at me.

"Good idea," he says. "Let's bring the party in here. I'm sure the nurses won't mind."

Nana Abu's face breaks into a slow smile as I move forward to give him a hug.

9

"All right, let's do this!" I say.

Nana Abu is sitting on the recliner and resting his legs on a small stool next to Zara.

"You remember what the physical therapist said, right?" Zara asks him.

"Yes." Nana Abu grimaces.

"Okay, let's do the leg raises first."

She pulls the stool out of the way so Nana Abu can lift each leg up and down ten times.

"Look at me, Nana Abu," I say. "I have to do my exercises too."

Ever since Nana Abu got out of the hospital last week, he and Naano have been staying at our house. Mama said it would be easier for everyone to chip in and help take care of him. I think she also wants to have him near us. We all do.

It seems as if Nana Abu is moving in slow motion, although he's moving at his normal pace.

"One . . . two . . . three . . . ," he counts in a raspy breath.

"One . . . two . . . three . . . ," I say, rotating my ankle as I stick out my leg.

I went back to see Dr. Alam yesterday, and he said I'm healing well. I don't have to wear the boot or use the crutches anymore. He gave me some stretches to do and said I can start to put weight on my foot and try to walk normally. That was the good news. The bad news is I still can't run or jump for two more weeks.

"Aren't you guys cute," Mama says as she walks into the room. "I knew getting the kids to work with you on your exercises was a good idea."

"After this we have to walk around the house three times," Zara says to Nana Abu. "You have to get in your steps."

"Maybe later." Nana Abu smiles.

"He should rest," Naano says as she shuffles into the room behind Mama. "You people need to leave him alone."

"He's been resting all day," Mama argues. "The exercises are important for his recovery. It wouldn't hurt you to do them too, you know."

It's weird to see Mama bossing around the oldest people in the house. I can't imagine telling my parents what to do, or them listening to me.

But Naano wins. Until we sit down for dinner.

"What is this?" she asks, wearing a frown as Mama puts out a big bowl of salad. "Where's the food?"

"Salad is food," Mama says.

"Salad is what food eats," Naano mutters. Everyone laughs except for Mama. Well, Baba kind of cough-laughs into his napkin.

"I have grilled chicken breast and steamed broccoli, too. After the salad. We need to eat more veggies and cut down on salt for heart health, right?" Mama stares at all of us.

"I love salad," Zara says smugly as she scoops some onto her plate.

Naano gives me a gigantic eye roll. I could kiss her.

Every meal has been similar to this for the past few days. Naano asks for salt and butter and Mama refuses, arguing that in her house they have to eat her food. Naano threatens to leave or to smuggle in parathas and extra-greasy halwa. Mama tries to ignore Naano, while we secretly give her thumbs up.

The best part of the bickering is watching Nana Abu smile through it all. It might be because he isn't wearing his hearing aid. But I think it's because he's happy to be home. I'm happy we get to do our exercises and complain about healthy food together. Later I might try to sneak us some ice cream.

10

I'm in the middle of naming my avatar in NBA 2K Wizzy the Wall-rus after my favorite basketball player, John Wall, when Baba yells from upstairs.

"Zayd! We're leaving in five minutes. Where are you?"

"Do I *have* to go?"

"Excuse me? Are you yelling to me from downstairs? Get up here."

I turn off the game and drag my feet up the stairs slowly. Not because my ankle hurts—because it doesn't. I'm just not in a hurry to leave.

"I don't want to go to the game if I'm not playing, Baba. Please?" I don't add how going to practice was miserable. I missed the last couple of practices and games because of Nana Abu getting sick. Now, since life is mostly back to normal, Baba is forcing me to go to the last game of the season. My team has to win to make the playoffs.

"We already talked about this." Baba frowns.

"Yeah, but . . ." I pause. "You don't know how horrible it feels to sit there and watch and not play."

Baba runs his hand through his hair and pauses before speaking.

"You remember when John Wall hurt his knee, right?" he asks.

"Yeah."

"Wasn't he there, for every game? Cheering on his teammates?"

"Yeah."

"And wasn't he still a leader?"

"I guess so."

"And isn't he your favorite player?"

"Yeah." I don't mention I was just naming my avatar after him.

"So get dressed already. Come on. No arguments."

"What should I wear? A suit and tie?" I figure if Baba wants me to imitate John Wall, I might as well go all the way.

"If you want. Whatever you wear, brush your teeth, please. There's some serious stench coming out of your face."

I put on an old basketball camp T-shirt and shorts and quickly brush my teeth. On the drive to the game, I think about what Baba said. John Wall is my favorite player in the NBA. Ever since I've been playing point guard, I've been watching his moves extra closely. I love the way he plays with heart and passion. And I suppose he's always there for his team.

But he also gets paid millions of dollars. He gets to be on TV. He doesn't have to go to school. There aren't thousands of fans waiting for me to arrive at the game. Plus, there aren't any cameras around, unless you count Chris's mom, who brings a gigantic lens to every game and takes a million pictures of her kid.

"Hey, Zayd," Coach Wheeler says as we walk into the gym. "Good to see you. How's the ankle?"

"Getting better," I say. "I should be back soon."

I start to follow Baba up the bleachers, but Coach points to the bench.

"Sit with the team."

I do what I'm told. Everyone else says "hey" to me when they come back to the bench after shooting around. As they crowd around Coach for the pregame pep talk, I stand awkwardly to one side.

"Zayd's going to take us out." Coach surprises me when he's done speaking.

Everyone opens up the circle, and I step forward to put my hand in the middle like I usually do for games.

"One two three . . . ," I say.

"MD HOOPS!" everyone shouts.

I look back at Baba, and he smiles at me from the bleachers. It does feel kind of good to be here. When I smile back at Baba, he knows I'm admitting it.

11

Coach Wheeler asks me to stand next to him during the game. Actually, he doesn't stand a whole lot. During all our games, he paces the sidelines and motions and sweats a bunch.

"Great rebounding!" he yells.

I can't keep up with him since I've just started walking normally again. So I stay in one place. But he keeps coming up to me and commenting on the game like I'm an assistant coach or something. I realize I never got to ask him about being the new team captain after I got hurt. Right now doesn't seem like the right time.

"We need to keep shooting while we're hot," Coach mumbles to me. I agree. Our team is on a run.

I felt a twinge of jealousy when Sam started the game at point guard instead of me. Now, a few minutes into the game, I can tell he's been working on his skills. He's moving the ball really well. We need to win to clinch our playoff spot, so everyone has to play their best, including Sam.

But if Sam plays *really* well, will Coach keep

him in my spot when I'm better? What if he picks him to be the new team captain?

"Subs!" Coach yells, and he puts in a couple of second-string players. Sam is still in the game, and my eyes are glued on him as I wonder what I would do if I was playing in his place. I notice all the good things he does. He has an awesome assist and a smooth no-look pass. I also see him rush a shot when he had time and flub his crossover.

One thing stands out on offense. Whenever a defender rushes at Sam, he looks to his right and passes to Blake on that side. A couple of times Blake had someone covering him tight, and he lost the ball. Meanwhile, Matthew was wide open on the left side of the basket.

This happens three different times, and the third time, the defender is anticipating Sam's pass and blocks it. It's right before halftime, and I'm sure Coach is going to point it out during the break. Instead he talks about other things, including everyone's energy level and remembering not to reach in on defense.

"We're up by eight," Coach wraps up. "But don't get fooled by the score. They're outhustling us, and we could be doing better. We need to finish strong if we want to do well in the playoffs. Let's give it our all this second half."

Coach has Sam take everyone out this time. I know I already had my turn at the beginning of the game. But it still stings a little bit.

Sam walks by me to put his water bottle back on the bench. I hesitate for a second, wondering what to do.

"Hey, Sam," I finally say.

"Hey." Sam looks at me.

"Good game so far."

"Thanks." Sam smiles and takes a sip of his water.

"I . . . um . . ."

I pause, wondering if I should say something about his passing or not. If Coach didn't say anything to him, why should I? He probably won't want to hear it from me. Besides, we're winning anyway.

"Yeah?" Sam looks at me and then at the court. It's time to go back on.

"Nice handles."

"Thanks." Sam's smile grows bigger.

During the second half, I try to squash the feeling of jealousy whenever Coach praises Sam. I make sure to yell extra loudly for everyone else on the team when they do something well. We pull out the win, and everyone is grinning at the end of the game. I'm happy too, because it means our season isn't over. But I down look at my foot and pray it's better in time for me to return for the playoffs. I'm dying to get back in the game.

12

"No, no, no, not that way. This way." Aliya, Mama's friend's daughter, hops as she flicks out her hand.

A line of girls, including Zara, are standing behind her and trying to mimic her actions. It's not working, and they're all doing the moves at different times.

"Okay, now show me." Aliya turns around and watches them. She doesn't say anything as she watches but kind of groans.

"Let's skip to the next part. We're going to be in a line. Move your hands like this." Aliya demonstrates.

A group of kids are crowded into our family room, where the coffee table is pushed out of the way. We're practicing dances for Jamal Mamoo's mehndi, which is on Friday night, only three days away. Zara insists we need at least three planned dances, based on the last one of these singing-and-dancing henna parties we went to. I don't think she remembers how the people at those parties could have easily been professional Bollywood dancers, not a bunch of kids who've never danced desi style before.

The worst part is the first dance is a cheesy love song. Zara thought it would be cute to include it. Aliya is the only one who speaks Urdu and understands what it's saying, so she's in charge of deciding the steps.

"At this part, when it says 'you're my heart and my life,' put your hands over your heart and make it thump like this."

Zara and the other girls look at one another. I wonder if Zara is thinking it's a mistake to have Aliya call the shots. I do. I watch while Zara nods her head and goes along and copies the moves. THUMP. THUMP. THUMP. It looks ridiculous.

Aliya's younger brother, Sulaiman, is the only guy who is almost as into dancing as she is. He doesn't seem to mind prancing around and pretending to be one of the dudes in love who act like fools in Naano's favorite Pakistani dramas. But he's seven.

Musa, a seventh grader who was probably dragged here by his parents, is sitting on the side next to me, watching with eyebrows raised.

"I'm not doing that," he says.

"Me neither," I agree. "I can't jump around. Doctor's orders."

"You can walk, Zayd," Aliya says. "But Sulaiman and Musa, you two jump."

"Not happening," Musa says.

Sulaiman looks slightly disappointed but says, "Yeah, let's do something else."

"We already agreed on this!" Aliya throws up her hands. "Do YOU have any better ideas?"

"How about we do a mash-up of songs?" I suggest. The idea just pops into my head. "We can use some of Jamal Mamoo's favorite hip-hop songs and mix them with Bollywood. What are those old-school movies he said he watched with Naano when he was a kid?"

Zara looks doubtful at first but then starts to get excited.

"I know a good mash-up app!" she says.

"Wait, wait. What about THIS dance?" Aliya glares at everyone. "We already worked so hard on it. I have all the steps done."

"I think this will be easier, and Jamal Mamoo will love it. We can do one big mash-up song instead of three different ones and be done," Zara soothes. "Is that okay?"

"Fine." Aliya doesn't look happy about it at all.

I get to work picking out the songs. I throw in "Heart of the City" by Jay-Z, since we always listen to it when we play 2K, and a bunch of my uncle's other favorites. Zara runs upstairs to ask Mama for the names of old Bollywood songs they listened to as kids. Within an hour

we have a professional-sounding mash-up. Aliya finally gets into it too.

Next comes the dancing part. Somehow I end up being the one in charge, probably since I'm the one not dancing. I throw up some music videos on Zara's tablet and piece together a dance, picking out the coolest moves from each clip. Surprisingly, it feels like I'm coaching and designing basketball plays.

Except the plays involve people jumping past one another instead of making jump shots and spinning around in a circle instead of trying a spin move to the hoop. Either way, everyone listens to me, and it actually comes together.

"My legs hurt," a girl named Fatima complains after we've been at it for another hour.

"I need water," Musa says. He wipes sweat off his brow.

"Okay, how about a fifteen-minute water break before we do it one more time," I suggest. "Let's give it our all until the end of practice."

As the words come out of my mouth, they sound familiar. I suddenly realize exactly who I sound like: Coach Wheeler! I can live with that. If I'm half as good of a coach as he is, this dance is going to be epic.

13

"Come on, Abu, please?" Mama is leaning over Nana Abu, who is sitting in his favorite chair.

"Maybe later," Nana Abu mumbles.

"But you didn't do it yesterday, either. The doctor says—"

"I will later." Nana Abu cuts Mama off. He

settles back into the recliner, pulls a throw blanket up to his chin, and falls asleep.

Mama looks at me and sighs as she walks into the kitchen.

"I'm worried about him," she whispers.

"What's the matter?" I feel dread spreading inside me. "Is Nana Abu sick again?"

"No. But he's not motivated to exercise. He hasn't showered, and he's sitting around in his pajamas. It's not like him."

"Maybe he's tired," I say.

"I know, but the doctor said it's important for him to keep moving."

"Is he going to be okay?" I ask.

Mama looks at me and forces a smile.

"Of course he is, sweetie. You're right. He's probably just tired. You want a snack?"

"No thanks."

Mama starts rummaging through the fridge,

but I head back into the family room and watch Nana Abu snoozing for a few minutes. I suddenly have an idea and go upstairs to look for Zara. She's in her room wearing headphones and doesn't hear me until I'm almost yelling her name.

"WHAT?" she yells back.

"I. NEED. YOUR. HELP."

Zara frees one of her ears. "I'm busy," she says.

"It's for Nana Abu," I add.

That works. Zara gives me her full attention while I tell her my plan. We head to the garage and start to search through boxes of junk.

"Here it is!" I hold up a dust-covered bat. This isn't any old bat. It's a cricket bat Nana Abu used to play with on his team when he was young in Pakistan. He gave it to Baba ages ago, but no one has used it in years.

"Nana Abu!" Zara and I race into the family room. "We need you!"

"What is it?" Nana Abu opens his eyes slowly.

"I'm trying to show Zara how to bowl, but she's doing it all wrong. She says she's right. But I know I am!" I hold up the bat.

"You're playing *cricket*?" Nana Abu is fully awake now.

"Yeah. I know all the rules from watching matches at your house. Zara and I want to play. Can you help us?"

In cricket, which is similar to baseball, bowling is the same as pitching, except you hit the ground with the ball and make it bounce. Cricket players hold the bat upside down, and there are things called wickets instead of bases. Players go back and forth between two wickets and can score hundreds of runs in a game.

"I was captain of my cricket team," Nana Abu says, not moving.

"I know." Zara tugs on his blanket. "That's why we need you to teach us. Please?"

"Where?" Nana Abu looks reluctant.

"Right outside."

"Well okay. I have to change my clothes." Nana Abu gets out of the chair and shuffles to the guest room. Ten minutes later he returns in a tracksuit.

We head outside to the lawn.

"Watch this," Zara says. She runs as fast as she can and hurls a tennis ball into the grass about two feet in front of me. I'm standing, holding the bat the way I would position a hockey stick. The ball rolls to my feet and stops.

"No, no, this won't do." Nana Abu shakes his head. "We need a hard surface."

"Can we go down to the little park and play

on the basketball court?" Zara suggests.

"Yes, all right," Nana Abu agrees. "But first show me the ball."

I hand Nana Abu the tennis ball, and he grips it in his right hand.

"See how my fingers are? Try holding the ball like this. And the most important thing is your follow-through."

"Like in basketball?" I ask.

"Yes."

As we walk to the park, Zara gives me a secret high five. We got Nana Abu to change his clothes and exercise! And he didn't even realize it because he was playing his favorite sport. Even though I still prefer basketball, cricket might be my second favorite. Especially if I get to play with my grandfather.

14

"We're on next," Zara announces. Her pink outfit is sparkly, and she's wearing a jeweled clip in her hair.

We're gathered around a dance floor in front of the small stage at the mehndi where Jamal Mamoo and Nadia Auntie sit on a carved bench swing. Red, gold, and dark green curtains are hanging behind them. Their fancy outfits match the colors of the decorations. Low tables filled with candles and trays of henna are arranged around their feet.

"Actually the aunties want to go next," Zara says as a bunch of older ladies get up and crowd the dance floor. I watch as they tug on Naano's hand, trying to get her to join them. She shakes her head and crosses her arms. Naano doesn't dance.

The deejay plays some song I don't recognize, and the aunties form a big circle. I can't help but think of basketball, the way they all put their hands together in the middle like my team does. Except they pull their hands up and put them back in again over and over. In between, they snap and clap and touch their elbows as they dance around. The thought of my team doing that makes me smile.

"They didn't practice," Aliya whispers to us. "They're so out of sync."

"They're aunties." Zara shrugs. "They're having fun."

Everyone claps politely for them when they finish, but they don't seem to notice. They are too busy congratulating themselves. Next it's our turn.

"Come on, everybody!" Zara says. Everyone gets in position, and I give the deejay the signal to start.

I'm nervous we won't be able to pull it off and worry everyone will forget the moves or the order of the songs. Every time a new part of the mash-up begins, someone has to use a prop—a pair of sunglasses or a wig or a scarf. When you add in the dance moves, it's a lot to keep track of. My job is to coach, and I only have a small part where I do a goofy walk into the middle of the dance floor wearing a hat over my eyes.

The music begins, and everyone is perfect to start. As in they are seriously killing it! I'm proud of them and steal a look at Jamal Mamoo and Nadia Auntie. They are clapping and cheering.

The grand finale is a Hindi song called "It's the Time to Disco" that has some English lines in it. We bust out some ridiculous moves that make Jamal Mamoo start to cry from laughing so hard. Then, as the last song ends, I run up and grab him and Nadia Auntie from the stage and pull them onto the dance floor.

"That was AMAZING!" Jamal Mamoo yells to me over the music. "I'm so impressed. Thank you guys for doing that!"

I grin at him. We pulled it off! Jamal

Mamoo and Nadia Auntie start to sway to the music. Suddenly mamoo's friends sneak up from behind and pick him up by the legs. He puts his arms in the air and waves his hands around as everyone hoots.

I see Jamal Mamoo point at me, and—WHOA!—the next thing I know I'm being

hoisted up onto some big dude's shoulders. I have no idea what to do, so I stick my hands up the way mamoo does and try not to fall off.

Zara runs over to Nana Abu and pulls him off his seat, and they dance together. Naano actually gets up too, and the two of them hold one of Zara's hands each and laugh while they slowly move to the beat. When I get back down to the dance floor, everyone boogies their hearts out. I manage to hop around a little, and my ankle doesn't hurt.

"I think I can play tomorrow!" I yell to Baba, pointing to my ankle. Tomorrow's our first playoff game. "Dr. Alam said I can play when I feel ready."

He gives me an "okay" sign while he does an awkward Punjabi dance move, acting like he's screwing in an imaginary lightbulb.

"We're going to do the traditions now, so

come on up and let's see how much mithai we can feed these guys!" the deejay announces.

Jamal Mamoo and Nadia Auntie settle back on the bench swing. Mamoo wipes the sweat off his forehead using a big dinner napkin while everyone crowds around them. The aunties place a dab of henna paste onto a big leaf on their hands and offer their congratulations. We all watch as they take turns feeding them Pakistani sweets. Jamal Mamoo obediently opens his mouth each time, even when the giggling ladies try to cram in huge pieces of mithai.

"Help me, Zayd!" he begs. "I'm going to gag." I stand next to him and convince the aunties to feed him M&M's instead.

After the rituals are over, it's time for family photos. Mama and Baba and Naano and Nana Abu come up to the stage and sit on either side of the bride and groom. Zara and I kneel in front. Nadia's parents come up too. Next her aunts and uncles and cousins and others I don't know join the crowd. It feels like a hundred people are squeezed onto the stage.

After my face hurts from smiling for pictures, I escape with Zara back to the buffet area to get a drink and some more of my favorite butter chicken. Dancing made me hungry. The food is already gone, but there's a bunch of desserts spread out on the tables now. SCORE! Along with mithai and rice pudding, there are plenty of cupcakes, too. When Jamal Mamoo and Nadia Auntie went to taste wedding cakes, they couldn't decide on a flavor, so they decided to get them all in cupcake form. Genius.

I devour a chocolate caramel cupcake and half of Zara's white chocolate raspberry one. I can't decide which one is better. Between the food, dancing, and seeing everyone so happy, this night was incredible. Plus, I'm finally ready to play.

15

I throw on my basketball uniform and strap on my high-tops. The Jordans Jamal Mamoo gave me when I first made the gold team feel as good as ever. I've kept them clean, so they look almost new.

"How you feeling?" Baba asks. He looks

tired. We got home late last night after the mehndi finally ended, and it's only eight a.m. I had a hard time waking up too. Mama and Zara are sleeping, so we crept around downstairs and ate cereal as quietly as we could.

"Pretty good," I say. I hop up and down a few times to test out my ankle. "Like normal."

"All right, great." Baba grabs a hat to cover his bedhead, and we get in the car. My stomach starts to clench a little, the way it always does when I'm nervous. I wonder what Coach is going to do about letting me play. I've been out for four weeks and missed practice and the last four games. Will he still start me in our first playoff game? I hope so.

Everyone looks as nervous as I feel when we gather around Coach for a pregame talk. The Badgers are a team we haven't played before, so we don't know anything about them.

"Okay, boys, I need everyone to play smart. You've worked hard all season, and it comes down to this," Coach says. "If we win this game, we're in the championship."

Then he gives us the starting lineup. I hold my breath, and . . . he says he's putting in Sam as starting point guard. I bite my lip.

"Zayd, you'll sub in for Sam. You let me know how you feel. Okay?"

"Sure, Coach. I feel good," I say, trying not to show disappointment on my face.

I start the game sitting on the bench, so I focus on figuring out the other team. They've got a couple of enormous kids, and their point guard is quick. But they look beatable.

In the first minute of the game, Sam makes a sweet move and passes the ball to Blake for a jumper. It's good! A few seconds later Matthew steals the ball from one of the tall kids, takes it down on a fast break, and makes an easy layup. I'm itching to get in the game and keep looking at the game clock.

After the first four minutes, we're up 6–4. Coach finally calls for subs, and I literally leap off the bench. Sam slaps my hand as he jogs off the court. Ravindu inbounds the ball, and I start to work my way to half court.

It feels great to be back in the game. But as I dribble, I suddenly become extra aware of my ankle. It doesn't hurt or anything. I just keep picturing my X-ray and the drawing of the ligaments inside my leg as I move. What if my ankle isn't fully healed? What if I twist it when I make a cut? What if I fall again?

I see a lane where I could drive to the hoop but pass the ball to Blake instead. He takes a jump shot and bricks it. Coach grimaces a little, but he doesn't say anything.

The Badgers score on their next possession. We're tied now. I get the ball back and pass it to Ravindu when a defender approaches me as soon as we cross half court. He takes a shot from close to the three-point line and airballs it. The ball rolls out of bounds, and I hear Coach yelling for a time out.

"Sam, you're back in," Coach says. "Ravindu, don't rush your shots. You guys need to calm down."

The whistle blows, and I head to the bench, but Coach stops me.

"What's up? Your ankle bothering you?"

"No," I say. "Not really."

"You're hesitating and playing timid. We can't afford for you not to give a hundred percent right now. You understand, right?"

"Yes, Coach."

"Let me know when you're ready go back in," Coach says.

I sit down and feel my face burn a little. I thought I was ready to play. I *am* ready! Although as I watch Sam hustle up and down the court, I notice how he goes all out when he runs. He doesn't seem to think about getting hurt the way he dives for the ball after an attempted steal pops it loose. I have to admit it reminds me of the way John Wall will do anything to make a play.

Right before the half ends, I notice Sam does the same thing as last game: He passes to Blake on the right and misses an opportunity to find Matthew open on the other side. We're down by two and are in a must-win situation. So this time I decide to speak up during halftime.

"Hey, Sam." I tap his arm and take a deep

breath. "Listen. I . . . um . . . noticed you pass a lot to Blake on the elbow."

"Yeah?" Sam squints his eyes, waiting for me to continue.

"And Matthew was open on the left. So try to look to for him, too, if you can."

Sam frowns slightly.

"Okay." He finally nods. "I didn't see him."

I notice that during the second half he takes my advice and doesn't make the same mistake again. It feels good to make a difference. I finally go back in and play better than I did in the first half. I make a good assist and one shot off the backboard.

Blake throws up a fist as the buzzer sounds.

We win 33–29 and are in the championship finals!

As we celebrate, Sam gives me a big high five. Coach pats me on the back.

"It's good to have you back, Zayd," he says.

"I like the leadership you're demonstrating."

I wonder if Coach overheard me talk to Sam. Maybe it will help convince him I should be team captain next season.

I won't lie: It feels really good to be back, and I'm glad I helped my team out. In the finals, though, I have to do better, a whole lot better. If I'm supposed to lead my team, I need to find a way to put my injury behind me and truly bounce back.

16

Adam's mom cries about everything. I've seen her cry during diaper commercials. She cried when she picked us up on the last day of school last year. Somehow she even managed to cry during our end-of-season party when Adam was still on my basketball team.

My mom? She's the opposite of Adam's mom. It takes a lot to make her cry. It takes even more for Naano to shed a tear. Today, the day of Jamal Mamoo's wedding, they are both crying buckets. It's kind of freaking me out.

It started this morning when we had breakfast and talked about the mehndi on Friday.

"I can't believe you and Abu danced together," Mama said, sniffling. "It was the most beautiful thing I've ever seen."

"Well, who knows how long we have left, right?" Naano joked, jabbing her elbow into Nana Abu's side. "We might as well dance for the first times in our lives."

She was kidding, but it made Mama cry harder. Naano's eyes filled up too. Then Jamal Mamoo, who was getting dressed for the wedding at our house, came out in his groom's outfit, and the tears started flowing again.

"Don't laugh, Skeletor," mamoo warned. He was wearing a long, stiff, embroidered jacket and white pants with gold threads on the edges. Best of all, he had on slippers that curled up in the front like a genie's lamp while he gave me an "I dare you to make fun of me" stare.

"You're a prince!" Mama exclaimed between sniffs. As corny as it sounds, I had to agree.

"Or a king, Mamoo," I said. "For real. I dig the shoes."

And now we're lined up to enter into the wedding hall, where the imam is waiting to perform the marriage ceremony. Mama is fixing the flower that's pinned on Nana Abu's jacket and wiping her eyes at the same time. Nana Abu looks handsome, like an older, grayer, less fancy version of Jamal Mamoo. I never noticed before how much they look alike.

We wait for Nadia's cousin to announce us over the microphone, and file in as all the guests watch. Zara and I are first up. I manage to get down the aisle without tripping while Zara practically skips. Mama and Baba are next, holding hands and blushing. And then King Mamoo walks in, standing extra tall, with Naano and Nana Abu on either side of him. He heads over to the decorated stage, where the imam is standing. They hug and turn to wait for Nadia's family to enter.

A couple of little girls throw flower petals on the ground, and then the bride makes a grand entrance. Everyone in the crowd stands up and murmurs their approval. She's a sparkling queen in cream and gold, the perfect other half to Jamal Mamoo. I see Mama wiping her eyes again as Nadia Auntie takes her place on the stage next to mamoo.

"Asalaamualaikum." The imam starts speaking. He talks about the beauty of marriage in Islam and the meaning of love, and asks each person in the room to ask for blessings for the marriage. When he finishes, everyone in the audience says "ameen" in one voice.

I try not to fidget on the stage as I wait until it's time for my job—handing Jamal Mamoo a ring. He takes it, says a few words, and puts the ring on Nadia Auntie's hand. She does the same in return. Then we stand there and wait and . . . nothing happens.

"Dude, aren't you supposed to, like, kiss the bride?" I whisper to Jamal Mamoo. At least I think I'm whispering. I guess I'm louder than I meant to be. Or maybe everyone else is super quiet. Jamal Mamoo turns red and lets out his wacky laugh. Nadia Auntie starts to giggle. Soon everyone starts cracking up. I'm not sure why, because I'm completely serious.

"How about they . . . ahem . . . celebrate in private later," the imam says with a chuckle. "But in the meantime, everyone please join me in congratulating the new couple!"

Jamal Mamoo takes Nadia Auntie by the hand, and they walk out of the room while everyone stands and cheers. We all go into a long hallway and eat tiny samosas and chicken pakoras passed around by waiters in tuxedos. Finally we go into a big ballroom, where round tables are set up with the gold fortune cookie boxes on everyone's plates. There's a long table on a stage set up for the bride and groom and their families, including Zara and me.

"Zayd, what were you thinking?" Mama exclaims when she corners me in the ballroom. "Have you seen kissing at other Pakistani weddings?"

"I guess not. I was thinking of TV weddings."

"This is a little different. And besides, Naano and Nana Abu would totally flip out," she adds.

"Yeah. I didn't think about what all the old people would think," I say.

We both pause, imagining. Then Mama starts to laugh and pulls me into a big hug. I see tears in her eyes, but they are the happy kind.

"I love you. Isn't this a wonderful day?" she says, looking over at her father. "I'm so grateful we could all be here together. And now I finally have a sister."

I give her a quick hug back and don't say anything because her words make me tear up too. In a good way. But just a tiny bit.

17

"Oh man, our worst nightmare. It's the Lightning," Ravindu groans as we walk into the gym together for our final game of the season: the championship!

"Are you surprised?" I ask. The Lightning are fierce. They always make it to the finals.

"No." Ravindu frowns. "But I wish it were someone else."

"We've beaten them," I remind him.

"I know." Ravindu still looks worried as he eyes the team warming up in their training shirts. I hide the fact that my insides are doing little flips and that I wish we were playing anyone else but these guys too.

"Good luck," Zara says. She gives me a fist bump and heads to the bleachers with my parents. Naano and Nana Abu made it out for the game too. Mama had tried to tell Nana Abu they didn't have to come since the bleachers would be uncomfortable.

"No," he'd said. "I'm going to see my grandson be a champion."

And now he takes a seat near the front, in his tracksuit and aviator sunglasses. He's the essence of cool. Jamal Mamoo wanted to come too, but he and Nadia Auntie left early this morning for their honeymoon in Florida. He texted Mama to wish me good luck and sent a million emojis of basketballs and trophies and a guy surfing, who I guess is supposed to be him.

Adam's already here, sitting next to his dad. He's wearing his old MD Hoops jersey, and it means a lot to have him here. My nerves kick into high gear when I think of everyone who came out to watch me. I have my own little cheering section on the bleachers.

"Zayd!" Coach calls me over to him. "How you feeling?"

"Good."

"Think you can start?"

"Yes, Coach!"

YES!

"I need you bring it strong. Can you do that?"

"Yes, Coach." I wonder if he can hear my heart pounding.

"Okay, let's do this."

Coach calls us all into a huddle.

"This is it, guys. This is the championship. You guys worked hard this season, overcoming injury . . ."

Everyone looks at me when he says that.

". . . and stepping up when you were needed . . ."

Everyone looks at Sam when he says that.

". . . and playing with your heart and your heads. I'm proud of you, no matter what happens in this game. Although I know you can win this. Focus and play smart. Are you with me?"

"Yes, Coach!" we all say.

"Zayd, take us out," Coach says.

We put our hands together.

"We got this!" I say. "One two three . . ."

"MD HOOPS!" everyone yells.

"Good luck," Sam says to me as we walk onto the court.

"You too," I reply.

"How's your ankle?" Sam asks.

"All better," I say. I'm not just saying it. I mean it. This morning I was up early, doing drills and shooting free throws on my driveway, and it felt perfect.

Coach is starting Sam at shooting guard. We haven't played together in a while. Today we need to be in sync and unstoppable, the way John Wall and Bradley Beal are when they find their rhythm.

I look around at Blake, Ravindu, and Matthew before sizing up the other team as we warm up. They are gigantic—like they each grew an inch since the last time we played them. Their point guard has a scowl on his face that resembles a cartoon villain so much it's almost funny.

I try to ignore how big they are and how good I know they are. Instead, I focus on the game as the buzzer sounds and we get ready for tip-off.

18

THWACK!

Number seven on the Lightning smacks the ball as I hold it up to make a pass. I'm being smothered by the defense. I manage to get the ball away and make a high pass to Blake. He dribbles and gets the ball to Matthew on the inside. I hold my breath as Matthew backs into a defender and turns to make a jump shot. It hits the rim and . . . it goes in!

We're down by one point, and the score has been up and down for the first seven minutes. Coach's shirt is already soaked in sweat, and he has been yelling nonstop. We're trying to keep up, but the Lightning are hot.

"It's too close," Sam says as we run back to defend.

I look at Coach to see what he signals. He's motioning for us to press harder. These guys are scoring no matter what we do on defense.

We double-team their gigantic point guard, but he burns us with his crossover. He gets the ball down to his power forward, who puts it in for an easy layup.

Coach calls time out.

"Okay, forget the press. Stick to the two-three zone. Zayd, you have to protect the ball while it's in your hands. Don't give them any chance to steal."

The referee blows the whistle, and we run back onto the court. I move the ball, looking for an opportunity to score. I've missed two shots already and haven't put up any points. It's already nine minutes into the half. I can't go scoreless!

I get past my defender, and Sam dishes the ball to me for an open pull-up jumper right inside the three-point line. It hits the rim and bounces right into the raised hands of the tallest kid on the Lightning.

ARGH! What's going on?

In the next three minutes the Lightning score twice. We turn the ball over once and get fouled. Ravindu goes to the line and makes one and misses one.

I'm shocked by how fast time is going by when the buzzer sounds at the end of the first half. We're down by six, and the Lightning lead. I can't believe I haven't scored. This is not at all how I imagined my return.

We all huddle around Coach, panting and chugging water.

"You're still in this," he says. "Don't let being down get to you."

I gulp some water and turn my head to the stands to where my family is sitting. Mama and Zara wave at me. Baba looks totally stressed out. Naano is talking to the lady next to her. Nana Abu has taken off his sunglasses. He catches my eye, raises his arm, and makes a fist.

Last night, when I said good night to Nana Abu, he pulled me close to him.

"You know, Zayd, when I was captain of my cricket team, we played in our championship tournament. I was very nervous about the other team. My father said something to me I never forgot," he said. I waited as he fell silent, lost in his thoughts.

"What did he say?" I asked after a few moments.

"What was I saying?"

"What your father said, before the championship game?"

"Ah yes." Nana Abu smiled. "Your great grandfather said, 'Don't let what you *can't* do get in the way of what you *can* do.'"

I didn't know what he was talking about and only pretended to agree that it was amazing advice. Now I think I finally understand what he meant.

I turn my attention back to Coach. As soon as he finishes speaking, Adam stands up and yells from the bleachers.

"LET'S GO, GOLD!"

Everyone cheers and gets fired up. Coach has Ravindu take us out. I can tell Ravindu's still nervous, because his voice squeaks as he counts, "One two three . . ."

"MD HOOPS!" I shout. I glance up into the stands again. Mama and Zara give me thumbs up. Baba points at me and yells, "Go, Zayd!" Naano is still talking to the lady next to her. Nana Abu gives me a knowing look.

I nod back at him and jump up and down a few times to get myself pumped before I run onto the court.

19

We start the second half with the ball. I call for a screen. Matthew runs over to set the pick and creates an opening in the lane. I take a step, pull up, and miss the shot.

"Don't rush, Zayd!" Coach yells from the sideline. I don't look at him, because I know I could have set that up better. My shot is still off, and I feel myself starting to panic.

The Lightning miss a three-pointer and Blake grabs the rebound gets the ball back to me. I head down the court again and see another shooting opportunity. I hesitate, pump fake, and WHACK. The defender hits my arm and gets the whistle. I'm up to the line for two.

Every player has a ritual before shooting free throws. I always dribble twice and picture the oil-stained spot next to the crack on my driveway where I practice.

DRIBBLE, DRIBBLE, BOING!

No way! It bounces off the rim!

DRIBBLE, DRIBBLE, SWISH!

It's good!

Finally! I put up a point, although I still haven't scored a field goal. I can hear my family cheering in the bleachers and Adam whistling. As I run back on defense, I can't help but think about all the mango milkshakes, rides to practices and games, one-on-one on the driveway, 2K battles, building my new basketball hoop, and trips to the doctor. It's like I can feel Nana Abu, Coach, Adam, Mama, Baba, Jamal Mamoo, Zara, my teammates, and friends carrying me, pushing me further, echoing my great grandfather's advice:

"Focus on what you *can* do, Zayd."

My shot may be off, but I can keep trying while I concentrate on defense, passing, and everything else I can do for now. We're still down 22–19 and only have six minutes left to play.

Over the next several minutes I turn it on and do my best impression of a determined

John Wall who's down in the fourth quarter. I hustle and have a couple of impressive passes and a few nice assists. I finally break the shooting slump and make a quick layup, a shot from inside the three-point line, and a pull-up jumper.

With a minute left in the game, I have seven points, three assists, a steal, and a rebound. It's much better than my first-half performance, but it's not enough to give us the lead. At least I know that no matter what happens, I've given it my all and done everything I can do.

The seconds are ticking by and we're down 28–27. It's our possession, and I pass the ball to Sam. He gets it knocked out of his hand by a defender. My heart sinks as I imagine the Lightning going on a fast break. Then Sam dives for the ball and manages to get it back! He tosses it to me, and I find Ravindu open. Ravindu drains the open shot.

"WOO-HOO!" I hear Zara scream.

And now I can't believe it—we're up by one! But it's the Lightning's ball, and they just need to score to win it all. Our entire season comes down to this play.

With twelve seconds left, the Lightning point guard looks confident as we cover them tight in man-to-man defense. It's as if we are gnats he can ignore. He passes it to number ten, who makes a move and blows by Sam.

But I'm quicker than number ten. Any thought of my ankle is history as I sprint down the court. I chase him down from behind. Then, right as he goes up for the layup, SMACK!

My block sends the ball soaring into the bleachers!

As the buzzer sounds, I'm smothered by my teammates in a gigantic group hug. I think we're jumping up and down in circles, or maybe it's the room spinning because it's hard to breathe. Either way, it's awesome.

I hear my family and Adam yelling and, when I look up, I see Adam standing and clapping. Naano and Nana Abu are beaming. Zara is doing a goofy dance. Baba is hugging himself. Mama is holding out her phone, and a tiny Jamal Mamoo is on the screen, hollering something I can't hear. I'm guessing he's yelling "Way to go, Skeletor!" I can't wait to tell him about my block and re-create it for him when he gets back. I'm going to relive this moment as often as I can.

Coach Wheeler comes around and gives

me a huge pat on the back that almost sends me flying forward.

"Incredible hustle out there, Zayd. That was some block," he says.

I'm already fired up and feeling confident, so I take a deep breath and decide to take a chance and ask for another thing I've been waiting for.

"So, Coach, do you think I could maybe be team captain next season?"

Coach frowns. He looks me up and down, like he's sizing me up. He scratches his head, and then starts to shake it slowly. I'm about to melt into the floor when he looks up at me and winks.

"Absolutely. You got it." He punches me lightly in the shoulder.

YES! I'm so overwhelmed and happy I can barely get the words out as I thank him.

I'm going to be captain of the gold team! The championship-winning gold team!

Then, just when I think the moment can't get any better, I hear my team chanting "MVP! MVP! MVP!"

And they're talking about me.